GHOST OF HEROES PAST

OTHER WORKS BY
CHARLES REID

Hurricanes over London
(Ronsdale Press, 2001)

Chasing the Arrow
(Beach Holme, 2004)

Ghost of Heroes Past

Charles Reid

RONSDALE PRESS

GHOST OF HEROES PAST
Copyright © 2010 Charles Reid

RONSDALE PRESS
3350 West 21st Avenue, Vancouver, B.C., Canada V6S 1G7
www.ronsdalepress.com

Typesetting: Julie Cochrane, in Minion 12 pt on 16
Cover Art & Design: Nancy de Brouwer, Massive Graphic
Paper: Ancient Forest Friendly "Silva" (FSC) — 100% post-consumer waste,
    totally chlorine-free and acid-free

Ronsdale Press wishes to thank the following for their support of its publishing program: the Canada Council for the Arts, the Government of Canada through the Canada Book Program, the British Columbia Arts Council, and the Province of British Columbia through the British Columbia Book Publishing Tax Credit program.

Library and Archives Canada Cataloguing in Publication

Reid, Charles, 1925–
    Ghost of heroes past / Charles Reid. — 1st ed.

ISBN 978-1-55380-102-3

    1. World War, 1939–1945 — Canada — Juvenile fiction.
2. World War, 1914–1918 — Canada — Juvenile fiction.
3. Collishaw, Raymond, 1893–1976 — Juvenile fiction. I. Title.

PS8585.E4485G56 2010   jC813'.6   C2010-901671-8

At Ronsdale Press we are committed to protecting the environment. To this end we are working with Canopy (formerly Markets Initiative) and printers to phase out our use of paper produced from ancient forests. This book is one step towards that goal.

Printed in Canada by Marquis Printing, Quebec

*This book is dedicated
to my grandson Charlie and
the thousands of other
young Canadians, in the
hope that it will help
them understand who
they are*

ACKNOWLEDGEMENTS

My thanks to all the people and organizations below, each of whom contributed to this book: Bill Chong; Geoffrey Marston; Ruth McIlrath; Elizabeth and Edwin Ride; the 1st Special Forces Association; the Devil's Brigade (USA); the Canadian Nurses Association; the Department of Veteran Affairs, Canada; the Vancouver Island Military Museum; and the Canadian War Museum, in Ottawa.

Although the principal protagonists in this book are fictional, the stories of military actions are as recorded, either by military archives, or as told by the actual participants in interviews with the author. Special thanks are due to those people for sharing their sometimes painful memories.

Chapter 1

"I THINK IT MIGHT BE a good idea for us to attend the Remembrance Day ceremony this year."

The total unexpectedness of his father's words were like a thunderbolt, and all Johnny Anders could do was sputter, "But Dad, that's my birthday."

"That's exactly why I think we should go. After all, you were born on a very historic day, Johnny, and don't you think we owe it to those men and women who gave so much for us, to spare them an hour of our time?"

"Yeah, but it's all old stuff that happened a long time ago. What's it got to do with me?"

"It has a lot to do with you. Those men and women and

what they did are the reason we are able to enjoy the life we do today."

Johnny rebelled inwardly at the thought of spending his fourteenth birthday standing around watching some old men going on about something that happened so long ago. He was not quite ready to give up, and tried one more protest. "But Dad, it's just going to be a lot of old people talking about stuff that means nothing to me. Anyway, we don't fight wars any more."

"Well, bad news for you: you have just given me a perfect example of how much you have to learn. It may have escaped your attention, young man, but there are a lot of our men and women, some not that much older than you, fighting in a place called Afghanistan right now. Now everyone might not agree one hundred percent that they should be there, but most people agree, at least, that we should support them while they are there. And one way to do that is by going to that ceremony."

A stubborn look had come into his father's eyes that Johnny knew all too well. With a sinking feeling, he realized that although his father hadn't actually insisted that Johnny accept his idea, further protesting at this time would get him nowhere.

As soon as supper was over that night, Johnny took off to his room, claiming he had a homework assignment. But when he closed his door he flung himself onto his bed.

Staring at the ceiling, he racked his brain for a way out of this disaster that had befallen him. He had to admit that he indeed knew almost nothing about the war in Afghanistan, let alone the two world wars and the other wars that were fought in this century and the last one. The truth was that he usually found himself daydreaming in history class — in all his classes, to be exact. His teachers' words seemed to float over his head and he was often caught staring into space. He became the butt of many jokes made by his teachers and classmates. He was shy and he had few friends — and even fewer A's on his report cards.

But going to the Remembrance Day Parade on his birthday would not make him feel any better. Briefly he considered pretending he was sick, as he had done several years ago to get out of a party for a girl named Maize Bledsoe, whom he couldn't stand. But just as quickly he dismissed the idea, muttering to himself, *Yeah, but I was just a kid then. It would be stupid now. Anyway, they'd probably do the same thing,* the "same thing" being that his parents had insisted he stay in bed all the next day to make sure he got over the illness. Johnny had long since figured out that they had known all along he was faking and had just kept him in bed as punishment.

When his mother put her head around the door to remind him it was getting late, Johnny was no closer to a solution that would prevent this shadow from hanging over his birthday. After getting into bed, he lay for a long time staring out his window into the darkness.

It was the smell that brought Johnny awake — a bitter, acrid smell of burning that filled the bedroom. Bolting upright, he became aware of a figure standing silently at the foot of the bed. Although it was dark, he could see the man quite clearly and realized that the smell was coming from the tattered uniform he wore. His first feeling was one of terror, and yet there was something emanating from this apparition that told Johnny he wasn't in any danger.

Suddenly the man stretched out a blackened hand. Astounded at himself, Johnny climbed out of bed and meekly took it. But as startling as all this was, it did not prepare him for what came next. The man led him toward his bedroom wall and then straight through it.

Before Johnny could even exclaim at this impossibility, he was shaken by the sound of explosions and the sight of flames shooting up into the night sky. He became aware that he was standing on a balcony overlooking a strange city. Curiosity overcame his fear and astonishment, and he whispered to the man, "Where are we?"

"We are in Hong Kong. It is December 1941 and the city has just fallen to the Japanese."

Johnny wasn't so ignorant of history that he didn't know Japan had been an enemy in the Second World War, but his knowledge of what had gone on in Hong Kong was zero. He was just about to ask another question when he realized they weren't alone.

On the far side of the balcony he could just make out a

short but powerful-looking man who was leaning over the railing and staring down into the street. "What is he looking at?" Johnny whispered.

"You don't have to whisper. He can't hear us. Go over and see for yourself."

As he reached the railing, Johnny heard a plaintive cry.

"Water, please, some water."

Leaning over, Johnny made out the figure of a soldier on the ground. A building at the end of the street suddenly burst into flame, lighting up the man, who was obviously badly wounded. But what startled Johnny more was the insignia on his shoulder: "Canada."

As he turned to ask the soldier-ghost about the insignia, he saw the short man who had been watching straighten up and stride toward the door behind him. But before he could go far, he was brought back to the railing by shouts from the street below.

Both he and Johnny craned forward and saw a group of soldiers running toward the wounded Canadian.

"Japanese soldiers," the soldier-ghost explained.

The Japanese surrounded the soldier, and one, an officer, reached behind him to where a water bottle was hanging. But to Johnny's horror the man's hand reappeared holding a pistol. Without a trace of emotion the officer pointed the pistol at the wounded Canadian's head and pulled the trigger.

The short man and Johnny both recoiled at what they

had just witnessed. But whereas Johnny's reaction was horror, the man's appeared to be fury; he slapped the railing hard and strode angrily through the door.

Johnny looked enquiringly at his soldier-ghost.

"He's angry because he is also Canadian."

This surprised Johnny. With the light from the burning building illuminating the balcony, the man looked like he was of Chinese origin.

The soldier-ghost answered Johnny's unspoken question. "He was born in Vancouver of Chinese parents and his name is Bill Chong."

"What's he doing here?"

"His father died while in China on business. As the number one son, Bill was sent over to look after the funeral. Unfortunately for him, by the time he had got through all the red tape, the Japanese already controlled the sea, and Bill had no way to get back to Canada."

"What will he do now?"

"Nothing immediately. But what he just saw will spur him to try to escape Hong Kong and get back to Canada so that he can fight in the war."

"Will he succeed?"

"Not in the way he expects."

"How then?"

"We will have to wait and see. For now, I want you to see something else."

With that the soldier-ghost took Johnny's hand again, and suddenly they were standing in a fenced compound with dilapidated huts scattered around its perimeter, except for one that was in good condition and flew a Japanese flag.

Near a large gate stood a sentry hut. A half-dozen soldiers who Johnny now understood were Japanese lounged against the hut laughing among themselves.

Suddenly there was a banging on the gate. Two of the soldiers walked over and flung it open. Another group of soldiers, all chattering excitedly, came in through the gate pushing a piano. They stopped and began talking to the sentries while pointing at it.

With all the commotion, other men began drifting out of the huts. But Johnny quickly realized these men were not Japanese soldiers. Some, he could see, were wearing the remnants of what had once been uniforms, many of which were in worse condition than his soldier-ghost's.

"They are Canadian prisoners of war, captured when Hong Kong fell to the Japanese," said the soldier-ghost, once again anticipating Johnny's question. "And this is a prison camp in Hong Kong called North Point."

"Hey, Geoff, come see. The Japs just brought in a piano."

The voice that interrupted the soldier-ghost came from one of the prisoners, who was shouting back toward the hut he had just left.

Another man, taller than most of the others, appeared in the doorway.

"Come on, Geoff, give us a tune," the other prisoners yelled.

The man walked hesitantly over to the piano, keeping a

watchful eye on the Japanese soldiers. Lifting the lid, he tin-kled the keys. Suddenly, all the soldiers became excited. One of them pushed the stool that they had brought in with the piano over to the Canadian and joined in the chorus of yells coming from the prisoners.

Geoff sat down and started to play. None of the songs meant anything to Johnny, but they obviously did to the prisoners, who all started to sing while the Japanese danced around excitedly, waving their rifles in the air.

The music went on for several minutes as the pianist moved smoothly from one song to another. Then the door to one of the larger huts was flung open and a Japanese offi-cer appeared, barking an order to the sentries. Immediately Geoff stopped playing and everyone fell silent. Another barked order and the soldiers pushed the pianist off the stool. Then both the stool and the piano were trundled over to the officer's hut and maneuvered inside, leaving the pris-oners to drift disconsolately back to their huts.

The soldier-ghost's voice broke the silence. "The pianist is a man named Geoff Marston. He's from Oshawa, in Ontario, and came out with the Royal Rifle Regiment, who were part of the Canadian battalion sent here to help the British defend Hong Kong. He plays in a local band back in his hometown."

"Why were the British defending it anyway?"

"Because at this time, Hong Kong is a British protectorate. They leased the land from the Chinese years ago."

"I don't understand. These Japanese soldiers here seem

pretty friendly, but then that officer we saw just shot a wounded man."

"Don't be deceived by what you just saw with the piano. These soldiers can be just as cruel. See that post there?" The soldier-ghost pointed to a wooden post, sticking about six feet out of the ground.

Johnny nodded.

"Well, those same soldiers use that for amusement. They will pull anyone off the street, tie them to that post, and keep jabbing them with their bayonets until the unfortunate person dies of his or her wounds. It is a favourite practice of theirs, and one you may see."

Johnny shuddered, shaking his head in disbelief at the thought of such cruelty.

His soldier-ghost continued. "Unfortunately, as you just witnessed from the balcony with the Canadian soldier, war can bring out the worst in people as well as the best, and not just on one side of any conflict."

"Do we torture prisoners?" Johnny sounded shocked.

"It is against the rules of war, and generally we don't. But remember that there is no such thing as a nice war, although there are some naïve people who would have you believe that a war can be fought without anyone getting hurt, and that the innocent can be completely protected from the turmoil."

"So, sometimes our guys do bad things, too."

"Sometimes, yes. No one, no matter what his — or her —

background, can avoid becoming dehumanized by war, because everyone fighting wants to win, and to win you usually have to kill many soldiers on the other side. In the case of these Japanese soldiers there is an added factor."

"What?"

"The harsh way they themselves were treated."

"How was that?"

"Well, they didn't get looked after the way soldiers from our part of the world did. When they went into battle, it was generally with only what they had on their backs, with few or no supply lines to reinforce them. They were expected to survive on what they could take from their enemies. This made them indifferent to suffering. Any man or woman unfortunate enough to be taken prisoner experienced some very harsh times. However, I think you've seen enough for your first night," the soldier-ghost said gently.

Taking Johnny's hand, he led him away.

Chapter 2

AS JOHNNY AWOKE, he realized that the bitter smell had gone. His head swivelled around the room. Everything was exactly as it had been when he went to sleep. Then his eyes shot over to the bedroom wall. It looked like it was as intact and solid as it always had been.

Slowly he got out of bed and went to the wall. He touched the spot he had walked through with the soldier-ghost. Or had he? He shook his head to clear it. *It must have just been a dream*, he said to himself, not very convincingly. After staring at the wall for a while he gave it a thump, then went to go brush his teeth.

"Johnny?" His mother's voice brought him out of his reverie.

"Yes, Mom?"

"Are you going to play with your breakfast all day? I have to leave for work in ten minutes."

"Sorry, Mom."

"You're not getting sick or anything, are you?"

"No, Mom." Johnny smiled at his mother, aware that if she started asking questions he might blurt out something about last night. He did not want to have to try and explain his strange dream to her.

After he had shovelled down his cereal, Johnny put on his jacket, grabbed his lunch and headed out into the grey November day.

Thoughts were flashing through Johnny's head as he trudged to school. *I could ask Mr. Gupta . . . No, that wouldn't work. He'd laugh it off. Well, what about Ms. Nowak? She's always been helpful and she's old enough to remember things like that.*

Fidgeting with impatience while pretending to look for books, Johnny watched as one student after another asked the librarian a question. Finally the last student left, and he shuffled over to Ms. Nowak.

"Can I help you? Oh, Johnny Anders, isn't it?" The librarian looked up as she spoke, a little surprised at who was standing in front of her. Johnny was not one of her regular visitors.

"Yes, Ms. Nowak."

"So, what can I help you with?" The librarian smiled encouragingly, aware that the boy was nervous.

"Is it true that a lot of Canadian soldiers were taken prisoner in Hong Kong by the Japanese in the Second World War?"

"Yes, that's true. They were sent over to help the British defend it. Unfortunately, it all proved useless as the Japanese overran the place very quickly and most of the troops became prisoners of war. The Canadians were interned in a terrible camp called North Point, which had been abandoned by the British years before for being uninhabitable. Is this a class project?" Ms. Nowak asked, her curiosity aroused by the boy's unexpected question.

But instead of answering, Johnny rushed on with another question that surprised the librarian even more. "Did you ever hear of a Chinese-Canadian named Bill Chong who was there?"

"Well, no, but I can tell you one thing. If this man was a Chinese-Canadian, he certainly wasn't in the army."

It was now Johnny's turn to be surprised. "Why not?"

"Chinese-Canadians were not allowed to join the armed forces in those days."

"How come?" asked Johnny, his curiosity now fully aroused.

"Well, the Canadian government had some pretty racist policies. Back then Chinese-Canadians were not considered citizens and weren't allowed to vote, even if they were born

here. Was this man connected with your family?" The librarian wondered where on earth Johnny had come by such information.

But Johnny, sensing that he was being drawn into a conversation that could force him to explain the reason behind
his strange questions, blurted out, "No, just something I
heard." Then with a muttered "thank you" he rushed out of
the library, leaving a speechless Ms. Nowak staring at his
departing back.

Later, as he trudged home, Johnny's mind was still spin-
ning with questions. "This is freaking crazy," he exclaimed.
"First Dad comes up with this weird idea about Remembrance Day and now I start having dreams about the Second
World War and I don't even know anything about it."

So you think it was just a dream then?

"Of course. It must have been a dream. Oh, this is just
great. Now I'm talking to myself."

But his inner voice would not go away.

Well, it's obviously true about Hong Kong.

"I could have read or heard about that somewhere."

And the Canadian soldier who was shot?

"Could have just been my imagination."

What about the prison camp? Ms. Nowak knew about that.

"All right, all right. I don't have all the answers. But it
must have been a dream."

Johnny shook his head, trying to stop these thoughts,
which were overwhelming him. "This is just freaking crazy."

"What's that, young man?"

The look of disapproval on the stern face of the old woman woke Johnny up to the fact that he had shouted the last words. "Sorry, ma'am," he mumbled. "I was thinking out loud." Then, too embarrassed to say anything more, he took off flat-out and didn't slow down until he reached his own front door.

That night Johnny's mind was still in turmoil, and he found himself wishing desperately for someone his own age he could confide in.

"Are you all right, Johnny?" his mother asked for the second time that day, as Johnny excused himself from the supper table.

"Yes, Mom. I just have to start my homework, that's all."

"If you say so," his mother conceded, not sounding convinced. Before she could say more, Johnny escaped to the sanctuary of his bedroom.

Homework? Stretching the truth a bit there, aren't we?

"It's not exactly a lie, is it?"

I suppose not. Well, the ghost may be coming back.

"We don't know that."

He said so.

Johnny slapped his forehead as he remembered his mysterious soldier-ghost's last words from the previous night. "He did say that was enough for my *first* night, didn't he?"

"Johnny? Who are you talking to?"

"No one, Mom. Just thinking out loud."

"Oh?" It was several seconds before Johnny heard her footsteps moving away.

Although full of apprehension at what the night might bring, Johnny was relieved to go to bed. At the same time, he was convinced sleep would never come. But he didn't realize the toll the turmoil in his mind had taken, and fell asleep quickly.

Chapter 3

THIS TIME WHEN THE smell of burning awoke Johnny, his eyes snapped open and went straight to the foot of the bed, where he knew the soldier-ghost would be standing. Seeing him there, Johnny found it harder to deny that the impossible was actually happening to him.

He stared at the soldier-ghost, hoping that he would disappear and everything would be normal again. But the ghost just stood there, his outstretched hand compelling Johnny to get up and take it. Unable to resist, Johnny rose, took the hand and walked through his bedroom wall.

They were standing in a jungle. The first thing Johnny noticed was a man crawling through a vegetable garden. There was a village in the background. Then he became aware of the Japanese flag flying from the roof of one of the huts.

As Johnny's eyes came back to the figure in the vegetable garden, the man turned around and began crawling in their direction. Johnny realized it was the man from the balcony: Bill Chong.

Reaching the cover of the jungle, the man sat down and rubbed the dirt off one of the potatoes he had been gathering. He started munching on the raw vegetable.

"Where are we and what is he doing?"

"We are in the jungle somewhere between Hong Kong and Free China."

"Free China?"

The soldier-ghost sighed. "I guess I'm going to have to do a lot of explaining as we go along. The Japanese invaded China some years before the Second World War began. Although they overran most of it, parts of the country are still in the control of the old Nationalist Party who formed the original government, and parts are under the control of the Communist Party. Each is fighting to get the Japanese out, but whereas the Nationalists want to restore the old order, the Communists want to get rid of the Nationalists as well. For now, however, they are united against a common enemy, even though they never mix with each other. Free China, as it has been dubbed by the Nationalists, is where Bill Chong is headed."

Johnny grimaced as the man took another bite of the

dirty, raw potato. "Doesn't he have any food?"

"No. It would have been too risky to carry food when he fled Hong Kong. Had he been discovered, the Japanese would have known what he was doing and arrested him. So he sold all his things and just carried money, thinking he could buy food along the way."

"Why can't he?"

The soldier-ghost jerked his hand at the flag. "He has found those flags flying at every village he has come to. It is a trick the Japanese employ. It is impossible to know whether there are soldiers in the village or not."

"Is the potato all he has to eat?"

"Yes, anything he can scrounge at night from these vegetable gardens."

"But will he make it to Free China?"

"Oh yes. In a few days he will arrive in the town of Kukong, tired and very hungry. But he will make it."

"But you said last night he doesn't get back to Canada. So what happens to him?"

"He will play a very important role in the war."

"What kind of role?"

"You will find out in time, but for the moment, I want you to see what is happening to our pianist friend in the prison camp. Come."

Johnny's soldier-ghost took his hand in the now familiar way and the two were back in the compound of North Point prison camp.

The rain was pounding down, turning the ground into a sea of mud. Suddenly a man appeared out of one of the small huts and staggered over to a larger hut. Johnny immediately recognized the man as Geoff Marston, who had played the piano.

Geoff made it to the hut and fell inside the door. The soldier-ghost touched Johnny's hand and they were inside the hut themselves.

The sight that greeted them reminded Johnny of a scene from a horror movie, except that he was becoming more and more convinced that this was all too real. Two rows of filthy iron cots ran down the length of the hut, all occupied by equally filthy men, who looked more dead than alive. A few men were moving around, wading knee-deep in dirty water that poured into the hut through the leaking roof.

Some of them were moving from bed to bed attending the sick, though they didn't look much different from the men lying motionless on the cots. Johnny guessed that they were doctors. The remainder were occupied in the odd task of beating the water with sticks. Taking a closer look at the muddy water, Johnny saw what he had not noticed earlier. Dozens of rats were swimming around, trying to climb onto the beds. Over everything hung the most awful stench Johnny had ever smelled.

One of the sick men, who had been lying so still that Johnny thought he was dead, suddenly stirred and dragged himself upright. An orderly helped the man from the bed, and with his support, the patient staggered to the end of the hut and into a small, doorless room. Johnny looked up at his soldier-ghost.

"That, for want of a better word, is the toilet, although what's really in that room is an old peanut oil can and an orderly to keep the rats away."

Johnny now realized where the stench was coming from and shuddered. He stood frozen before the whole horrific scene until he noticed Geoff Marston being laid on one of the beds. Then he found his voice. "He's going to die, isn't he?"

"Many of them will, but not him. He will be one of the lucky ones. We'll see our pianist again."

"What's the matter with them?"

"Most of them have contracted dysentery because of the terrible conditions they are kept in."

Johnny knew what dysentery was and immediately understood the reason for the stench.

The soldier-ghost roused him from his thoughts. "This is what I meant about the complete indifference of the Japanese to suffering. In cases like this, they don't deliberately set out to torture their prisoners. But the results can be the same."

"I still can't believe *our* guys would behave like that, though," Johnny said, referring back to their conversation of the previous night.

"No, they wouldn't in normal circumstances. But war is

not normal, and in the heat of battle, especially when things are not going well, anyone can react in ways they wouldn't even contemplate in peacetime. Come, I think you've seen enough."

"Why me?" Johnny said, blurting out the question that had been driving him crazy since the previous day.

"That you will come to understand for yourself, in time." And with that, Johnny had to be satisfied, as the soldier-ghost ended their journey for the night.

Johnny awoke the next morning and lay for a long time staring at his bedroom wall, his thoughts once more in turmoil. "So, now I'm supposed, in some magical way, to figure out for myself why this is happening," he mumbled. "How am I supposed to do that?"

So now you believe it's not just a dream.

"Oh God, I'm talking to myself again. But it's just so crazy. I mean, I'm wandering around the world somewhere in the past with a ghost. Jeez."

Well, so far he's convinced you it's not just a dream, so why not wait and see what happens next?

"Yeah, you're right. Anyway, I don't have much choice, do I? . . . I wonder why he showed me what was happening in that hospital. It was pretty gross."

Perhaps it's all part of what he wants you to understand

about war and Canada's role in it. Because that's what this is all about, isn't it?

"I guess. Wonder what he'll show me tonight."

So you're convinced now that he'll be back?

Johnny banged his head with his fist and jumped out of bed. "This talking to myself is getting more crazy than walking through walls," he muttered. Then, without a glance at his solid, seemingly impenetrable bedroom wall, he took off down the stairs.

Chapter 4

⬭

THE NEXT DAY AT SCHOOL was certainly not one of Johnny's best. Not that he was often blessed with good schooldays, but this one was particularly low on the scale.

He was reprimanded at least half a dozen times for not paying attention and twice threatened with being kept behind if he didn't wake up. This was extra frustrating because, for once, Johnny was wide awake. It was just that his mind was consumed with what might lie ahead that night. For now, having dropped all pretense that his strange experiences were just weird dreams, he had no doubt that the nightly visits would continue until this mysterious soldier-ghost had shown him everything he wanted him to see. Would he find out what happened to Bill Chong? How would Geoff Marston manage to survive his bout with dysentery?

When school was finally over, Johnny decided to visit the library to do some reading so that he wouldn't look like such an idiot when his soldier-ghost took him on the next nocturnal visit. The first book he found claimed to cover all the most famous battles from the two world wars. He started reading and quickly became engrossed in a section dealing with air warfare.

"My great-grandfather was a fighter ace in the Great War."

Johnny, who had become completely absorbed in the book, looked up with a start. He was even more startled when he saw the person who had spoken to him.

A freckled face, from which peered the most intense green eyes Johnny had ever seen, was surrounded by a mass of red curls escaping from a battered baseball cap. But it was not the face that surprised him the most. The body attached to the face was clothed in a shapeless, oversized t-shirt of no particular colour. The shirt hung over a pair of jeans that were so tattered that Johnny felt, had they been his, he would have thrown them in the garbage.

Johnny was still staring when the girl — at least, he thought it was a girl — spoke again. "I'm sorry I interrupted you." With that she began to turn away.

"No, no, don't go. I was just . . . I mean I didn't . . ." Johnny's voice trailed off.

The girl slid into the seat opposite him. "Are you interested in that period of history?" she asked, pointing to the book.

"Yes. No. Well, sort of."

The girl laughed. "Which is it?"

"Well, I wasn't before, but now I am."

"What brought it on?"

Johnny realized he would be getting into murky waters if he tried to explain his sudden interest. "Oh, just something someone told me," he said off-handedly.

The girl laughed again. "OK, I won't pry into your deep, dark secret. But if you're really interested, I have a lot of stuff at home, like on my great-grandfather and some other people. If you make up your mind about being interested, let me know. You'll find me in here most days."

With that, she gave Johnny a casual wave, got up and headed toward the door, leaving him staring at her back.

This strange girl was like no other he had ever met. Not that Johnny had met many girls of any kind. The ones at school barely gave him a glance, and certainly would not have wasted their time talking to him, he felt, except to deliver the occasional snide remark.

All the way home, and for the rest of the evening, Johnny could not get the girl from the library out of his head. His thoughts kept returning to her odd clothes. *I wonder why she wears gear like that*, he pondered, knowing from conversations he sometimes overheard between girls that clothes seemed to form a large part of their world.

In fact, for the first time since his strange experiences had begun, something other than his nightly trips with his soldier-ghost occupied his mind. His last waking thoughts were of the girl. So he was even more taken aback than he might have been, when, upon walking through the wall that night, he found himself looking at an entirely different landscape from the green jungles of Asia. He turned his eyes enquiringly to his soldier-ghost.

"We shall get back to our two friends later, but now we must move on. You have much to see before our time is over."

The soldier-ghost's words were not lost on Johnny, and confirmed what he had already come to expect. Still, he could not see why he was being given this insight into his nation's history. And what, if anything, he was supposed to do with it.

For now, he realized that he could only take it all in and hope that before it was over, he would come to see its purpose. His eyes turned to the scene confronting him.

Johnny found himself staring across what once must have been green fields but was now a quagmire of craters, mud, barbed wire and endless rows of trenches that seemed to go on forever until they became just blurs on the horizon. Over everything hung an eerie silence.

"It is 1917 and the First World War is being fought," the soldier-ghost said. "We are in France, on the Western Front. But the war has reached a stalemate, and this same piece of ground has been fought over for nearly three years already."

"Why? That's crazy."

"You see, when the German army swept into France in 1914, their plan was to push straight on to Paris. They calculated that the French would be forced to surrender. But their supply lines were stretched, and their commanding officer became nervous that they were at risk of the French and British armies counterattacking and cutting them off. With this in mind, the army was ordered to dig in and build a defensive line.

"The French and British did the same. Over the following months these lines became larger and more elaborate until each side had created such a strong defence that neither could break through. It is a mistake the Germans will not make almost twenty years later when they invade France again in the Second World War."

"So where exactly are we now?"

"We are standing at the Allied defence line, and over there are the German trenches." The soldier-ghost pointed to more trenches a short distance away, where the land sloped upward toward a hill.

"Are we going to see another Canadian hero?"

"Well, yes and no. That hill is called Vimy Ridge. At the moment, it is held by the German armies and has been a thorn in the Allies' side almost from the beginning of the war. As you can see, they have an unparalleled view and can detect any attack being made on them. The Allies have made numerous attempts to take the ridge — at great cost in lives. Now, it is the Canadians who are going to try, and it will prove to be the only time that four Victoria Crosses, Britain's highest award for valour, were ever awarded in a single day."

At that moment gunfire erupted, and Allied troops began pouring out of their trenches toward the German line of defence. To Johnny's surprise, the men marched purposefully toward the German trenches at a steady pace. He then realized that shells were exploding just ahead of them.

"It's called a 'creeping barrage,' and it helps protect the men from the German machine guns," the soldier-ghost explained. "But when they get close to the enemy trenches the barrage will have to stop in case it hits our own men."

Exactly as the soldier-ghost predicted, the creeping barrage stopped when the advancing soldiers closed in on the enemy positions. A hail of gunfire immediately erupted from the German lines. Many of the men, who had broken into a run, dropped to the ground. But none of those left standing stopped. They poured on across the open ground, through gaps in the barbed wire guarding the trenches or scrambling over it until they disappeared into the enemy trenches, from which emanated shouts and curses mixed with gunfire and screams of pain.

One group heading for the ridge was already scrambling up the slope when Johnny felt a touch on his shoulder and found himself standing on top of the hill looking down, as the soldiers surged upward. Another deadly hail of bullets came from the trenches, and many of the soldiers on the slope fell.

Two machine gun posts were exacting a particularly heavy toll, and the soldiers caught in their fire began to falter. Suddenly, one man from the Canadian side rose and started running toward the two posts, crouching low and weaving from side to side. Miraculously, the hail of bullets missed him and he reached the posts unharmed. Pulling a grenade from his belt, he yanked out the pin and flung the grenade into the first machine gun dugout. He followed it with another, which flew into the second dugout. Two explosions erupted almost simultaneously, and both machine guns fell silent. With a loud cheer, the soldiers further down the slope got to their feet and charged up the rest of the hill, pouring into the main enemy trenches behind the machine gun posts, the soldier who had silenced the two machine guns leading the charge.

Johnny was still staring in amazement when his soldier-ghost spoke. "His name is Private William Milne, and for that act he will become one of the four soldiers who will be awarded Victoria Crosses this day. That's what I meant when I said yes and no to your question about seeing another Canadian hero. Private Milne is just one of many heroes who will contribute to this battle."

"Do they win the battle?"

"Oh yes. They capture the ridge, and hold it against all German counterattacks. It will go down in history as both the Allies' first major victory of the war and Canada's greatest military achievement. Today, it is considered the moment your young country came of age. Unfortunately, Private Milne will not live to know what he contributed this day. He will be killed very soon."

Johnny sucked in his breath at the news.

"Tomorrow we are going to see war from up there." The soldier-ghost pointed skyward. "You will see how air power started to change the way wars were fought. You will also meet another Canadian, who not only becomes a hero in this war but goes on to serve in three more."

"Who is he?"

"His name is Raymond Collishaw and he was born on Vancouver Island. Now it is time for you to go home."

Chapter 5

THE FIRST THING THAT came into Johnny's head when he woke the next morning was the fact that his soldier-ghost had told him what to expect the following night. But almost as quickly came the thought of the strange girl he had met yesterday. *Wonder who she is, and why does she wear that crappy gear? She sure doesn't look like any of the other girls at school.*

He climbed out of bed and got dressed, the picture of the strange girl still in his mind, where it would remain for the rest of the day.

Johnny looked for the girl at every break throughout the day, but not once did he catch a glimpse of her.

After school, he thought about going to the library. Then, shaking his head, he turned for home. But after a few steps he stopped and looked back at the library. His inner voice started up again.

Well, make up your mind. Are we going to look for her or not?

"I thought maybe she might know something about this stuff. She said she had a great-grandfather who was a fighter pilot in the First World War."

So go look for her then.

Finally convincing himself, Johnny swung around and without any further hesitation strode toward the library.

He found her sitting in the same section they had met in yesterday, her head bowed over an open book. She seemed completely engrossed and yet, as Johnny approached, her head came up and she smiled.

"So, did you finally make up your mind?"

"Well, yeah. I mean, I would like to see your stuff."

"OK. When do you want to do it?"

"Well, I have to let my mom know. Could we do it tomorrow?"

"Can't tomorrow, I'm busy. The day after would be all right."

Johnny bit his lip. As his soldier-ghost had said he was going to show him something on air warfare that night, he was hoping this girl's "stuff" would help him get an understanding of it beforehand.

Sensing his hesitation, the girl said, "Tell you what. Why don't you go and ask your mom if you can come over now?"

"She won't be home from work until about five o'clock."

"Oh. Then why don't you phone and leave her a message? Then you can check back again from my place when she's home."

"Yeah, I could do that. Do you know where the phones are?"

"Don't you have a cell?"

"I'm getting one for my birthday," Johnny said, feeling sheepish.

The girl smiled and reached into her baggy jeans. "Here, use mine." She slid her cellphone across the table.

"Thanks." Johnny called home and left a message, saying he had gone to a friend's house and would call his mother again from there.

"Well, now that that's done, let's go. I don't live far. By the way, I'm Casey."

"Johnny."

The girl chuckled. "I know. You just said it on the phone."

Johnny grinned and smacked his forehead in a gesture of mock disgust. "'Course I did."

As they walked along, Johnny couldn't help casting sideways glances at the girl, until eventually she said, with a laugh, "I guess I'm not much like your usual girl, eh?"

"No, it's, it's not that," Johnny stammered. "It's just I was wondering if you were new, 'cause I haven't seen you before."

"We just moved here a month ago, and I only started back to school last week. Here we are."

Casey turned into the driveway they had just reached and headed for the front door, with Johnny trailing behind. As they entered, the smell of fresh coffee wafted down the hallway. "Come on, my mom must be in the kitchen. First thing she always does when she gets home is make herself coffee."

The contrast between Casey and her mother was startling. Casey's mother was elegantly dressed in an expensive-looking blazer and pants. She turned as the two came in, holding a cup of coffee in her perfectly manicured hand. She raised an enquiring eyebrow at the sight of Johnny.

"Mom, this is Johnny. He's interested in war history and I'm going to show him some of my stuff. Can I take him up to my room?"

Casey's mother smiled at Johnny, but her smile turned into a frown when she looked at her daughter. "Casey, do you have to dress like a bag lady? She does have decent clothes, you know," she said to Johnny. "How are you, Johnny?"

"I'm fine Mrs. . . ." Johnny's voice trailed off as he realized he had no idea what Casey's last name was.

"Collishaw."

Casey's mother could not have shocked Johnny more if

she had thrown her coffee into his face. He stood rooted to the floor, the hand he had put forward to take Mrs. Collishaw's stuck out straight in front of him as if it were encased in ice. He knew his mouth was hanging wide open but he couldn't make it close. *Close your mouth, idiot, and do something!* his inner voice shouted. But he couldn't move.

It was Casey who came to the rescue, by yanking on his other arm and saying, "Come on, let's go upstairs."

Once in her room, Johnny was presented with another shock. There were no movie star posters on the wall, nor were there any of the other girly things he had noticed in his cousins' rooms when he had visited their homes. Instead, model planes dangled from the ceiling and photographs of men in uniforms covered her walls.

"Would you like to tell me what the heck that was all about?" Casey had slammed her door shut and was looking straight at him.

He noticed a large portrait on the wall by her bed. It was of a man, smiling from the cockpit of a strange-looking plane with three wings, all mounted above the fuselage.

Johnny walked over to it and looked closer. "This is him, isn't it? Your great-grandfather, I mean."

"Yes, it is, but stop trying to avoid my question. Why did you freak when my mother told you our name? Johnny, answer me." Casey's vivid green eyes were burning into his.

"Uh, oh, that was nothing. I just read his name in that book at the library, so I was kinda surprised." Johnny thought he was off the hook, but he soon found out what a huge mistake he had just made.

Casey's eyes were now blazing and her hand was on the door handle. "Do you think I'm one of those airheads you're probably used to hanging out with, Johnny whatever-your-name is? I know every book on the Great War in that library and I know there's only one that briefly mentions my great-grandfather. So what's the deal?"

Johnny recoiled at the fury in Casey's voice and could only stutter, "I don't really know any girls."

"That's your problem. Now you have about ten seconds to tell me what this is all about. Otherwise, you're history."

Well, you've really done it this time. Let's see you get out of this one. Of course, Johnny had no more of an answer for Casey than his inner voice did, except the obvious one, which he dreaded. Yet he still stood there, unable to move, unable to speak.

But there was no escaping Casey's fierce gaze, which was fixed on him unwaveringly. "Five seconds."

When his time was up, Johnny did the only thing left he could think of. He ran. Blurting out, "Sorry, I gotta go," he tore toward the door and pulled it open, brushing aside Casey's hand as he did so. Then he rushed down the stairs, jerked open the front door and called out, "Bye, Mrs. Collishaw," as he flew down the driveway.

"Casey, what was all that about?" Mrs. Collishaw called.

Casey ran down the stairs to find her mother standing in

the hallway, her half-finished coffee in her hand, staring at the open front door. "Beats me, Mom. I was just asking him about why he acted so strangely when he heard our name, and suddenly he mumbles something, then takes off."

"What a strange boy."

"Weird, more like." Casey shook her head as she walked over to the front door and closed it.

Once he was halfway down Casey's block, Johnny slowed to a walk. Just then his inner voice started up. *Well, that was smart.*

"What else could I do? If I told her about the ghost, she'd think I was crazy."

And you don't think she does right now?

"OK, I panicked. But I still don't know what else I could have done."

Johnny trudged home, feeling more depressed than he had since his strange experiences had started. He realized that not only had he lost the chance to get some help understanding more about what his soldier-ghost was showing him, but more importantly, he'd lost the chance to make a friend.

Chapter 6

AS HIS EYES OPENED and he saw the soldier-ghost standing by the bed, Johnny's first thought was that whatever he saw tonight, he would still have no one to share it with. When they passed through the wall, he was shocked to see a number of odd-looking three-wing planes identical to the one he had seen in the photograph of Casey's great-grandfather. Johnny's annoyance with himself for his behaviour that day increased.

But when they moved toward the aircraft, his annoyance turned to wonder as he got a close-up of these planes, which were like none he had ever seen. Two things were distinctly different about them. Some had their nose and wheels painted red, some blue, and others black. He also saw that the planes painted black had names on the side. A step closer revealed that the nearest one was named "Black Maria."

"That one is Collishaw's plane." Johnny's soldier-ghost spoke for the first time. "Collishaw and the other Canadians that made up B Flight, or 'Black Flight,' as it became known, decided to give all their planes names, and it seemed natural to use names beginning with 'Black.' If you go closer, you will see that one is called 'Black Roger,' which belongs to a man named Ellis Reid; another that is called 'Black Death,' which belongs to John Sharman; a third that's called 'Black Prince,' which is William Alexander's plane; and the last one, 'Black Sheep,' which belongs to a man named Gerry Nash."

"Hey, that's cool. So this is a Canadian First World War squadron?"

"Not exactly. You see, Canada doesn't have an air force of its own at this time, so the Canadians are either members of the British Royal Flying Corps, more commonly called the RFC, or, in the case of the naval squadrons, members of the Royal Navy. The fact that Naval 10, this squadron, consists mainly of Canadians — there are eight of them — is pure coincidence."

"Oh." Johnny was a little deflated by this news, but came back with a further question. "If they belong to the navy, why are they here?"

"I thought you might ask that." The soldier-ghost smiled. "They have been sent to the Western Front to help bolster

the RFC, who have been getting pummelled in the air battles with the Germans. Morale is very low."

"And are they? Helping, I mean."

"Oh yes. In fact, they are succeeding almost too well, particularly this squadron and its Black Flight, which is the one
we are here to follow."

"How can they succeed too well?"

This time the soldier-ghost chuckled. "Well, not as far as
the Allied High Command is concerned, but they are proving so good that they are making the RFC look bad. The RFC
pilots have been complaining that they can't compete against
the Germans because the German planes are superior. But
that little tri-plane is a big part of the navy flyers' success,
and the RFC turned it down because they claimed it wasn't
good enough."

"Why are they painted different colours?"

"Well, unlike the planes in your world, these planes are
very light, which makes them quite unstable when taxiing on
the ground. A crosswind could tip them over, so the ground
crews have to run out and grab the wings as soon as they
land. The colours are to identify each flight to their respec-
tive ground crews."

Suddenly, several men in flying gear appeared from one
of some nearby huts and headed toward the planes. "Looks
as if we are going to see some action. Better get on board."

Johnny looked at the soldier-ghost in astonishment.
"We're going with them? How?"

"Oh, we'll just ride piggyback."

A touch of the soldier-ghost's hand and Johnny found himself riding behind the man he already knew as Raymond Collishaw as the plane rushed down the grass airstrip and climbed into the sky. In a panic he tried to grasp the fuselage but realized instantly that in spite of the rushing wind, he was not moving, and seemed to be anchored securely to the plane.

In a short while they were crossing the maze of trenches sprawled across the countryside below. After a few minutes, Johnny became aware that Casey's great-grandfather was signalling to the pilots of the other two planes flying with him. Following his signal, Johnny spotted two larger planes accompanied by three smaller planes, all marked with crosses. They were German bombers with a fighter escort. Suddenly, Raymond Collishaw put his plane into a steep dive, followed by his fellow pilots.

The German fighters broke away and climbed to meet their attackers, but the Canadians' quick dive carried them past the fighters and straight at the bombers. Collishaw speedily maneuvered himself into position on the tail of one. His machine gun began chattering deafeningly. The bomber burst into flames and began spiralling toward the ground, where it broke into pieces that continued to burn.

Before he could draw breath, Johnny became aware that bullets were hitting their plane from behind. Looking back, he could see one of the German fighters right on their tail, so close in fact, that Johnny could see the grinning pilot as he poured bullets into Collishaw's fuselage. But then the tiny tri-plane seemed to stand on its tail as it pulled up and away from the deadly hail of bullets. Then it turned sharply and rolled sideways. To Johnny's astonishment, the German plane was now right in front of them, the pilot frantically trying to get out of the position he had held Collishaw in just a few seconds earlier. But there was no escape from Collishaw, who followed his every turn as he poured his own stream of bullets into the German fighter. Then, just as the bomber had done a short time ago, the fighter burst into flames and plunged, crashing into the ground below.

Looking down, Johnny noticed that the other bomber was also lying on the ground, a mass of wreckage. One of the other two pilots was giving Collishaw the thumbs up, while the third pilot was furiously chasing the other two fighters, who had broken away and were heading back from where they had come. Fortunately for them a thick bank of cloud appeared. They escaped into its all-enveloping safety, leaving the third Canadian pilot thumping the side of his plane in frustration.

Raymond Collishaw signalled a return to base and soon they were taxiing along the grass airstrip, with ground crew members grabbing the wings as the planes came to a halt. In a few minutes, Johnny found himself back on the ground standing beside his soldier-ghost.

His heart was still pounding from the experience, and the

excitement was still in his voice when he spoke. "Do they do that every day?"

"Most days, yes, although they don't always manage to engage the enemy."

"This guy Collishaw is really good, isn't he?"

"Oh yes. In fact, there are quite a few of your modern historians who claim he was actually the top ace of this war, though officially that honour belongs to a German named Baron von Richthofen, more commonly known as the Red Baron, on account of his red plane. The top Canadian honour belongs to a man named Bishop."

"How come?"

"Well, all this goes back to what I was telling you earlier about how the naval squadrons put a flea in the ear of the RFC brass by proving they could compete with the Germans. Because the official tally of enemy planes destroyed — 'kills,' as they call them — is kept by the RFC, they stick to the rules rigidly when it comes to naval pilots, particularly ones as good as Collishaw. But they are more lenient when it comes to their own pilots."

"What do you mean?"

"Simple, really. The rules state that for a plane to be officially designated a kill, it has to be witnessed by two other pilots, who have to see it actually hit the ground. Now, as you just saw, it is very dangerous for pilots to hang around in order to watch a plane crash, so it's often impossible to meet this requirement. Therefore, although every one of

Collishaw's kills will be witnessed by two other pilots as going down in flames, the pilots will not always be able to confirm that they actually hit the ground. Because of that, quite a number of Collishaw's kills will be discounted. But this rigid interpretation of the rules is not always applied to the RFC pilots. For instance, many of Billy Bishop's claimed kills will not be witnessed by others, and will rely solely on his own account of them. This is not to say they are necessarily illegitimate, but it does reveal a double standard."

"That's a crock."

Johnny's soldier-ghost smiled. "I'm afraid that even in wartime things get deliberately distorted, especially when some high-ranking officer's reputation is at stake.

"On the plus side, Raymond Collishaw will have a very distinguished career, serving in four wars. He will retire as an Air Vice Marshal, the second highest rank in the Royal Air Force, which he also served in, and will become one of Canada's most decorated heroes. Come, I think you've had enough adventure for now."

Chapter 7

JOHNNY WAS STILL so frustrated with himself over the way he had behaved at Casey's the day before that he was paying even less attention than usual at school. Suddenly, he became aware that Mr. Gupta, his history teacher, was looking pointedly at him, and that all his classmates were looking in his direction.

"Well, Johnny?"

Johnny sat staring at the history teacher, not having the faintest notion of what he was expected to say.

"Asleep again, Johnny. I just hope you have grasped a little more about the Russian Revolution from past lessons than you appear to have done today. Because you have only until the end of term to produce your essay on the subject. Class dismissed."

Johnny walked out of the classroom nonplussed.

Sounds as if you better do some catching up, eh? Johnny's inner voice piped up.

"What do I know about the Russian Revolution?"

You might know something, if you hadn't been daydreaming in class for most of the term.

"Of course you can always try the library. That's what it's there for, you know."

Johnny groaned. The words were spoken by Jason Lee, who had obviously overheard Johnny talking to himself. *Just what I need,* he thought, as the class genius fell into step beside him.

"Very funny, Lee. I know where the library is and what it's for. I'm not as stupid as you think."

But Jason was already disappearing around the corner, and the words were lost on him.

Johnny stormed out of the school, angry with himself for letting Jason get to him. *Oh, if only I could tell him what I knew. That would wipe the smirk off his face.* But no, he would just become the laughing stock of the school.

He had managed to find Casey during lunch break, but as soon as she saw him she had taken off with some friends. As he began walking home, however, he bumped into her.

Casey, her eyes flashing, said, "You stay away from me Johnny . . . what is your last name, anyway?"

"Anders."

"Well, anyway, Johnny Anders, you stay away from me. You're crazy."

"Please, Casey, give me a chance to explain."

"Explain what? You running out of my house like you were a complete nut, and leaving my mom wondering if all my friends are weirdos?"

"But if I had tried to explain yesterday, you'd have thrown me out anyway."

"If you think I'm going to let you back into my house, you're even crazier than I thought."

"Of course not. But I thought if we went to the library I could try and explain. Please Casey, it's really important. For you *and* for me."

"Important enough to me that I have to listen to some weirdo?" But Johnny's words and his almost begging tone made her relent. "OK, you get ten minutes and it had better be good."

With that Casey turned and led the way over to the library.

Once they had found a quiet corner, Casey said immediately, "OK, let's have it."

Knowing he was on borrowed time, Johnny swallowed his fear and plunged right into the story of his strange experiences.

Casey sat quietly, her eyes fastened on Johnny's. They showed no expression until he reached the part about her great-grandfather and his amazing adventure of the night before. Then she threw up her hands. "Whoa, wait, my brain's already reeling. Are you telling me you actually hitched a ride on the back of my great-grandfather's plane as he went on patrol? How is that possible? You would fall off."

"That's what I thought at first, and I tried to hang on. But it was so freaky, Casey. I didn't need to. It was, like, as if I was stuck there, no matter what."

"Oh man, this is so bizarre. But go on."

Johnny told Casey the rest of his story. When he had finished, he sat back, exhausted, relieved and terrified all at the same time. *What will Casey do? Run screaming to the librarian, or just get up and leave?*

But as the minutes ticked by, Casey did neither of these things. She just sat there, her eyes fixed steadily on his as they had been throughout his strange story.

He could stand the suspense no longer. "You still think I'm bonkers, don't you?"

"Why did the soldier-ghost pick you? Are you some kind of a history nut?" Casey asked, ignoring his question. Then, before Johnny could speak, she answered herself. "No, of course you're not. Otherwise, you wouldn't need me."

Johnny laughed derisively. "Me, some kind of history nut. Don't I just wish."

Casey lapsed into silence again, still staring into Johnny's face, as if trying to find the answer to a puzzle. After Johnny had endured what seemed to him a lifetime of agony, she finally spoke again, answering his original question. "No, I don't think you're crazy, but you have to admit it's a heck of a story you're asking me to swallow."

"So, you don't believe me then?"

"I didn't say that either."

"What do you believe?"

"That no one, not even a nutcase, could come up with a story that included so much detail about my great-grand-father without knowing me first. And since we never met until a couple of days ago, that's just not possible. So, my new and very strange friend, as weird and unbelievable as your story is, I can't say it isn't true. Still, there's one thing I do know. If you actually rode with my great-grandfather on a mission, you have got to be the luckiest guy in the world. I would give anything to be you."

Johnny was taken aback. Until now he had looked on the strange happenings of the last few nights as more of a curse. But seeing what was akin to adulation in Casey's eyes, he began to understand, for the first time, that he was being given a once-in-a-lifetime opportunity to experience the past.

He was also aware that Casey half-believed him. His breath came out with a rush, making him realize he had been holding it in, waiting for an answer he was sure would be full of mocking disbelief.

"So, if this ghost of yours comes every night, that means he'll be taking you somewhere tonight, right?"

"He has so far."

"Then we'd better meet at my house after school tomorrow."

"But aren't you busy tomorrow?"

"I was, but that was before you told me your wacky story. Now there's no way I'm going to wait another day to hear about what happened to you, even though I still need to be convinced I'm not crazy just for listening to you. And talking about this at school would be stupid, for sure."

"Yeah, I guess it would. But what about your mom?"

Casey gave him a mischievous smile. "Guess I'm going to have to come up with a little story to explain yesterday. But don't worry, I'll think of something."

Johnny thought of how badly this day had started and could not help but marvel at how well it had ended, even though he knew that he was still on probation with Casey. Unfortunately, that thought also brought back the memory of what had happened in class today. His face fell as he remembered his impossible assignment.

Casey noticed the sudden change in him. "Hey, what's up? Why the sudden dark look? I thought you'd be relieved I didn't call the cops and have you locked away." In spite of her flippant tone, Casey looked genuinely concerned.

"I am, honest, but this has nothing to do with all that."

"OK. Spill it. I'm listening."

Johnny needed no more encouragement. He told her about the essay on the Russian Revolution his class had been assigned.

Casey was immediately all business. "Well, we'll have to put our heads together and come up with something, won't we?"

"You'll help me?" Johnny was flabbergasted.

"Why not? Like I said, there's no way I'm letting you go, at least until this whole bizarre story of yours comes to an end. If it all turns out to be true — and it's still a big 'if' — I'm going to owe you a big one for the story about my great-grandfather. And anyway . . ." Casey gave him a strange smile. "The idea I have, if it works, will mean we both get something we want."

Johnny shook his head in bewilderment. "I don't have a clue what you're talking about. But it's got to be better than any idea of mine, because I don't have any."

"Good. First we need to go back to my house, so that I can show you what I was going to show you yesterday, before you ran out like your pants were on fire."

Johnny gave a rueful smile. "I must have looked like an idiot. But what about your mom? You haven't told her yet."

"Oh, I guess I'll have to come up with something a bit sooner." Casey gave him a wink. "When we get to my place, you wait in the hall while I go and see my mom in the kitchen."

"Whatever you say."

Chapter 8

CASEY CAME BACK from the kitchen and smiled at Johnny, who had been fidgeting anxiously in the hallway.

"Come on, let's go upstairs and I'll tell you my idea for your essay."

"Is it OK then? What did you tell her?"

"The answer to the first question is, 'of course.' And the answer to the second one is, 'don't ask.'"

The pair went upstairs to Casey's room and shut the door behind them.

"OK. This is my idea," Casey said, flopping on her bed as she spoke. "My great-grandfather fought in the Russian Revolution, so why not do your essay as told through his eyes?"

"I don't get it. Why would he fight in a revolution in Russia?"

"Thought you might ask that." Casey gave Johnny a mischievous look. "Because the Czar, that is, the ruler of Russia at the time, was a cousin of King George the Fifth of Britain."

Johnny threw up his hands in despair. "You've lost me."

"OK, I'll tell you the full story. The Communists were trying to take over Russia, and the British government knew the King didn't want to abandon his cousin when he was in trouble. They also knew that if the Communists won, the British government would have to recognize them officially as the new rulers of Russia, and deal with them as they would any other rulers of a foreign country. They didn't want that.

"With all that in mind, the last thing they wanted was to make a complete enemy of the Communists. So they decided on a compromise. They sent just a few squadrons to Russia so it would look like they were helping the Czar, which made the King look good. But at the same time, by doing this, they were showing the Communists they had no real intentions of interfering with the revolution. My great-grandfather, who became a fully fledged officer in the British Royal Air Force after the first war ended, was put in charge of one of those squadrons."

"So he fought for the Czar against the Communists?"

"You got it."

"But if I'm going to write my essay using his experiences, where do we get the information?"

Casey smiled triumphantly as she reached over to a book-shelf. "From this."

Johnny looked at the book. The title read *Air Command: A Fighter Pilot's Story*. There was no mistaking the man on the cover.

"This is what I was talking about in the library yesterday."

"Where did you get the book?"

"My grandmother gave it to me before she died. She was one of his two daughters."

"Did you know that a lot of people who study this stuff believe your great-grandfather was actually the real top ace in the Great War, not this German guy they called the Red Baron?"

"Von Richthofen. Yeah, I know. Did your soldier-ghost tell you about it last night?"

"Yeah. What does your great-grandfather say about it in here?" Johnny pointed at the book.

"Almost nothing. I only know because my grandmother mentioned it. She said it was something to do with the air force people being jealous of the navy flyers."

"'Cause the navy flyers were too good, according to the ghost. Seems crazy to me. I wonder why your great-grand-father doesn't talk about it in the book?"

Casey's face showed a sense of pride. "From what my gran told me, he just wasn't that kind, you know, a bragger. He was more interested in winning the war."

"You know, I still can't figure out why I'm being shown

all this, instead of someone like you, especially with your great-grandfather and all."

"Maybe you should ask your ghost."

"I did, but all he said was I'd find out as I went along. The trouble is, I don't have a clue how. I mean, what do I know about this stuff?"

"I think you put yourself down too much, Johnny Anders. I don't think you're anywhere near as stupid as you keep saying. As for what it all means, I guess we'll just have to wait and see."

The word "we" was not lost on Johnny. But he made no comment, fearing that if he did, his new friend might suddenly vanish. Instead, he contented himself with asking her about something else.

"Casey, do you go to the Remembrance Day parade?"

"Every year. Don't you?"

"No, but my dad wants us to go this year. He said it's more important now, with our soldiers fighting in Afghanistan."

"He's right, Johnny. It is important, especially for them. It would be horrible for their morale if they thought we didn't care."

"Yeah, I guess it would be. So could we, like, meet up and watch it together?"

Casey grinned. "Hey, what's this? You beat me to it. I was just going to suggest the same thing."

It was at that moment that Johnny looked at his watch. "Oh jeez, I forgot to call my mom, and she'll be home from work by now."

Casey handed him her cell. "You'd better call her then, hadn't you?"

Johnny threw her a grateful glance, took the phone and dialed his number.

"Hi, Mom. Sorry I'm late. I'm with Casey and forgot the time."

"Who's Casey?" his mother asked. "I never heard you mention a boy named Casey."

"Casey's a girl, Mom. Not a boy."

"Oh." There was a pause. "A girlfriend. Well, that's new. You never mentioned a girlfriend." Johnny could almost see his mother's nose twitching.

"Aw, Mom, it's not like that," Johnny replied, as he noted the mischievous grin on Casey's face, who had obviously picked up on the gist of the conversation. "She's helping me with a history essay, that's all."

Casey made a face at Johnny and stuck her tongue out.

"Wow, a girlfriend *and* a sudden interest in history. Things are looking up."

"Mom, I told you, she's just a friend."

"Whatever you say, but this Casey must be quite something. Do I get to meet her?"

"I guess."

"I really do want to meet this person who can stir up your interest in studying. Anyway, you have about forty-five minutes till supper's on the table, so don't be too long."

"OK, Mom." Johnny put down the phone to find Casey grinning from ear to ear. "She was asking about you."

"I got the drift," Casey said, before bursting into laughter. Finally she composed herself. "So, do you have to get home?"

"Yeah, pretty soon."

"Well, why don't you take the book with you?" Casey held it out to Johnny. "And do some reading tonight. Then we can go over it tomorrow. That is, if you can stay awake. How do you stay awake anyway, with all this running around in the past?"

"You know, that's the funny part. I never feel tired the next day. It's more like I'm dreaming all this stuff, except I know I'm not."

"That's a relief. I don't want you falling asleep in my room one day. My mom might not be too keen on that."

An awkward silence fell over the room. Johnny stood up and began fidgeting with the book.

Casey gave a nervous laugh. "Hey, I wasn't serious. Just bugging you, that's all. Now get out of here, and take care of that book. Otherwise you'll be in big trouble."

Johnny gave an equally nervous grin. "You know, I'm really glad we met. I was going nuts over all this, and then this essay thing comes up. I didn't know what to do until now."

"Hey, if all this turns out to be true, it means we share the best secret ever. So that makes us best friends, too. And what are best friends for?"

"Yeah, I guess we are, aren't we?" He hesitated before blurting out, "See you at school tomorrow."

It was more question than statement, and Johnny waited anxiously for Casey's response. Would she want to be seen with the school loser?

But he needn't have worried, for Casey smiled. "Sure, if you want. We can meet up during lunch break."

"Oh, great."

"But we can't talk about all this. Otherwise, they'll be taking us both away."

"No, of course not."

"Good. Now get going, or you're going to get it from your mom."

All the way home, Johnny kept repeating the words over and over. *Best friends. That's what she said: best friends.*

Chapter 9

"SO, TELL ME ABOUT this girlfriend."

"Girlfriend! Johnny has a girlfriend? Since when?" Johnny's father put down his knife and fork, and looked with curiosity from his wife to his son.

"It appears Johnny has found himself a girl, and one with brains, too," Mrs. Anders replied, her eyes twinkling.

Johnny stopped eating and said, "Don't be gross, Mom. I told you she's not my girlfriend. She's just a friend who's helping me with this history essay I have to do."

His father chuckled. "Oh, that's a new one. I never came up with an excuse like that."

"Peter, stop it, and let the boy speak." Mrs. Anders gave

her husband a look of mock disapproval.

Johnny's father turned back to his son. "History, eh? That's interesting. What part of history?"

"We have to write about the Russian Revolution."

Johnny's father whistled. "And how are you going to set about doing that? And where does this girl come in? Is she an expert or something?"

"Not exactly. She had a great-grandfather who was a famous fighter pilot in the First World War, and he also fought on the side of the Czar in the Russian Revolution."

Johnny's father was all ears. "Did he now? I never knew any Canadians served in Russia."

"He was actually in the British air force. King George the Fifth was a cousin of the Czar, and when the king heard about the revolution, he wanted to help. So the British government agreed to send fighter squadrons to Russia to fight the Communists, and Casey's great-grandfather went as a squadron leader." Johnny paused for breath.

His father was staring at him, astonished at his son's grasp of something he himself knew nothing about.

Johnny couldn't stop the thought from jumping into his head: *Got you there, Dad, didn't I?*

"And this girl told you all this. Where did you find out about it?"

"In this book." Johnny reached behind his chair to the cabinet, where he had placed it. "It was written by her great-grandfather."

Johnny's father took the book and looked at the cover. "This him?"

"Yeah."

"By the look of his uniform, he was well decorated."

"He was. He was one of the best fighter pilots in the war. Some people say he was the best." Johnny felt a warm glow spread over him as he tossed out his newly discovered knowledge. He almost felt like a history teacher himself.

"So, how is this going to help with your essay?" Johnny's mother asked.

"Well, it was Casey's idea. She said I should tell the story of the revolution through her great-grandfather's eyes."

"Ambitious. Do you think you can do it?" There was a look of doubt on his mother's face.

Johnny, his voice full of a confidence he didn't really feel, replied, "Yeah 'course I can. Casey says there's a whole section of the book about it and I should be able to write it pretty much as it happened. And she's going to help me."

"Well, this is one smart girlfriend you seem to have found yourself. How come we've never heard of her before?" Johnny's father asked.

"Because she hasn't been here that long. Her family moved here just a month ago. Anyway we only just met," Johnny said, deciding he was wasting his time trying to convince his parents that Casey wasn't his girlfriend.

"So, how did you meet her?" Johnny's mother spoke up again.

"I was in the library reading this book about the First World War, and she came up and asked me if I was interested in this stuff."

"Well, however it happened, anyone who can get you seriously interested in studying any subject is good for you, and gets my vote." Johnny's father sat back with a pleased look on his face.

Oh thanks, Dad, Johnny thought, wondering how his father would react if he knew that his son was getting a history lesson like no other.

"I agree, and would love to meet this girl," Johnny's mother said. "Why don't you invite her to supper on Saturday?"

Johnny knew this was coming but could not stop the doubt from creeping into his face as he wondered what his parents would make of Casey who, with her old, grungy clothes, would be starkly different from any girl they had ever met.

But his mother misinterpreted the look. "She's not one of those, what do you call them, you know, the ones with purple hair and green lipstick, is she?"

"Punks, dear," his father cut in. "Personally, if she can get him interested in studying, I don't care if she has green hair and purple lipstick."

"No, Mom, Casey's not a punk. If you're worried about it, I don't have to ask her to come."

"Oh, no you don't. Whatever she is, I still want to see this girl who is turning you into a student of history."

Realizing this was more demand than request, Johnny just nodded.

Everyone got back to supper, and Johnny's parents didn't ask him any more questions. When the meal was finally over, he escaped to his room with the precious book under his arm.

Chapter 10

SETTLING DOWN AT his desk, Johnny opened the book. He soon found the section dealing with the Russian Revolution and began reading.

So engrossed was he in this story of a war fought across a vast country that surpassed his own in sheer size and brutal weather, that he didn't stir until his mother's voice brought him back to the present.

"Johnny? It's getting late."

"OK, Mom."

Reluctantly, he closed the book and headed to the bathroom to brush his teeth. It was only as he was climbing into bed that Johnny remembered his soldier-ghost and wondered where he would take him that night.

The all-too-familiar acrid smell of burning brought Johnny awake. As was normal now, he climbed out of bed, took his soldier-ghost's hand and walked through his bedroom wall.

So many things had happened to Johnny over the last few days that he had almost forgotten about Bill Chong and Geoff Marston in Hong Kong. So he was surprised to find himself back in the Asian jungles. This time, though, he was looking out across a huge expanse of water. He looked up enquiringly at his soldier-ghost.

"This is the South China Sea. It leads to the port of Macau and Hong Kong. See that old boat out there?"

Johnny became aware of a boat sailing in the distance.

"Macau?"

His soldier-ghost smiled as he realized the boy was as lacking in geography as he was in history. "Macau is what is known as a free port. It sits just across the bay from Hong Kong, in Mainland China. Although it is officially Portuguese territory, it operates pretty much by its own rules. That's where that boat is heading, and it has Bill Chong on board."

"Why is he going there?"

"Well, as Portugal is neutral in this war, it is also supposed to be outside Japanese control. Bill is going there to contact the British consul, who has been helping people escape from Hong Kong. Many of those escaping were senior people in the Hong Kong administration before the war. Because of their experience, they will be invaluable to the British government in getting the territory back functioning as quickly as possible once the war is over. Therefore, they want to bring them to safety. Bill has been given this task, in addition to that of carrying secret messages to and from the consul."

"You said *supposedly* outside Japanese control?"

"Ah, there's Bill's problem. The Japanese have recruited many Chinese who were friendly to them, and trained them into a private army known as the Kempeitai. They are all over Macau, particularly around the British consul's residence."

"So it's going to be difficult for him to get to the consul then?"

"Right. But before then, he is going to face another challenge. Let's go and see."

With that the soldier-ghost touched Johnny's hand and they were on the deck of the boat.

Looking around, Johnny realized that he was on a very old boat. In the bow was mounted a cannon that looked even older. From the boat's mast flew a Japanese flag.

"This boat belongs to a man called Cripple Kay, and he is one of the many bandits who operate along these coasts. Our friend Bill Chong has paid Cripple to take him to Macau. Cripple is gambling that the Japanese flag will fool the Japanese gunboats in the area into leaving them alone."

"And I guess they don't, do they?"

"You're getting smarter."

Johnny figured out which one was Cripple Kay by the man's deformed arm. But the only other people on the boat were two dirty-looking labourers.

"Bill's the one on the left. The other is Cripple's crewman. Pretty good disguise, isn't it?"

"I guess."

"Well, he's about to need it."

It was at that moment Johnny noticed the gunboat looming out of the mist. This boat was also flying the Japanese flag, but Johnny knew immediately this one did not belong to a bandit.

Cripple Kay, who also had noticed the gunboat, immediately cut his engine and let the boat drift, knowing that to continue forward would result in being sunk.

As soon as the Japanese boat came alongside, an officer jumped aboard followed by two soldiers. Brandishing a pistol, the officer barked something at Cripple Kay. Cripple's answer obviously didn't satisfy him, because he smashed the bandit across the face with his pistol, knocking him to the ground. Cripple stood up. The officer shouted again, and once more slammed Cripple to the ground. This routine went on for some time, with the officer asking questions and knocking Cripple down with his pistol every time he answered him.

Then the officer said something to his men, and they stepped forward, jabbing the three men with their bayonets and pushing them toward the entrance to the hold of the boat. Once Cripple, Bill and the coolie were in the hold, the door was slammed shut and locked. Johnny watched as the men on the gunboat fastened a line to Cripple's boat and began towing it toward shore.

"They're in trouble, aren't they?"

"Somewhat. Let's take a look in the hold and see what is going on."

In the gloom of the hold, Johnny noticed Bill Chong reaching into his tunic. He pulled out a pouch and, dropping it to the floor, began stomping it into the mud in the boat's bilge.

"That tobacco pouch is where he has all his papers for the consul. He knows that if he gets caught with them, he will certainly be tortured. Slowly and excruciatingly, until he's eventually killed."

"What will happen to them?"

"If we take a quick jump forward three days you'll find out." A touch from the soldier-ghost and Johnny found himself on land in a Japanese camp. As he looked around, the officer appeared with his men. They went over to a small, windowless hut. Opening the door, his soldiers dragged out three filthy, bedraggled men. So dirty were they that Johnny didn't recognize them at first, especially as they were all covering their eyes to shade them from the blinding sun.

Then all three were dragged back to Cripple Kay's boat, which was tied up at the dock, and thrown back into the hold. Locking the door, the officer gave his men another order and they cast off, towing Cripple's boat behind them.

"What are they doing?"

"Time to find out."

Immediately they were back on the deck of Cripple Kay's boat. Johnny watched as the Japanese soldiers towed it to the middle of the South China Sea. Then they cast it adrift and, gunning their engine, headed back to land.

Johnny looked up in amazement at his soldier-ghost.

"If you remember, I told you the Japanese have to find their own supplies because they don't get much help from their High Command, which makes them very careful about how they use them. Consequently, they avoid wasting bullets on people other than soldiers. Whenever they can, they just bayonet them. But it seems our officer has a twisted sense of humour, so he has cast them adrift to die instead. But he didn't reckon on the cunning of the old bandit."

A touch of the soldier-ghost's hand and they were back in the hold. As Johnny's eyes adjusted to the gloom, he noticed the bandit sitting in the mud and kicking at several planks of the boat's hull that were above the water line. After a few minutes, some of them sprang loose, and Cripple wriggled out, dropping into the water. Soon the door to the hold was flung open and there stood a grinning Cripple Kay.

He spoke to the two men, but they didn't need any orders. They ran up on deck and rushed to one side. The crewman fastened a rope around his chest and Bill took hold of the other end. The crewman slid over the side of the boat and quickly refastened the loose planks.

Bill Chong, though, had one last thing to do. He went back into the hold and, reaching down into the slimy mud, fished around until he finally came up with his precious tobacco pouch. Cleaning off the mud, the Canadian tucked it back inside his tunic.

Outside, Cripple Kay had already hoisted the ragged sail, and soon the boat began to move.

"Are they going to Macau?"

"No, not even old Cripple is that brave — or dumb — come to that. They are heading back to his base."

"So they'll be all right then?"

"Yes, but not before spending several more days without much food and water. The Japanese, of course, never gave them much while they were held prisoner."

"So does Bill Chong get to Macau and complete his mission?"

"Oh yes, and he goes on to make many trips back and forth, bringing to safety many important people and valuable intelligence about the Japanese and their troop movements. But we must leave Bill Chong's adventures for a while, as we still have much to see. We will visit him again before our time runs out, because I want you to witness another miracle escape of his. But for now, we need to pay our friend Geoff Marston a visit, to see how he is recovering. Come."

Instead of the filthy, rat-infested hut that served as a hospital in the camp known as North Point, Johnny found himself in a hospital that looked exactly like the ones in Canada. There were rows of beds covered with spotless white linen and nurses attending the men that occupied them.

"Bowen Road Hospital, Hong Kong," the soldier-ghost said. "You're wondering why the Japanese bring prisoners here to recover after they virtually kill them with their treatment in the camps. Well, as you have already seen, the

Japanese were a mass of contradictions all through this war. They never seemed to have any deliberate policy of extermination as the Nazis did, but mostly they were just as brutal as the Germans — perhaps even more so. It seemed to stem from a complete indifference to suffering or death when it came to their enemies or the people of the countries they overran. Yet keeping this hospital open for prisoners suggests the complete opposite.

"Having said all that, don't be fooled by what we are seeing here. Everything in this hospital is being done solely by the nurses and the handful of doctors, who became prisoners when Hong Kong fell. They are using medicines that were already here at that time. Their food rations are the same as in the camps, with everything divided into exactly the same portions for everyone, including the doctors and nurses. However, in keeping with the inexplicable behaviour of the Japanese, this will not last. Soon, they will close the hospital and everyone will be sent to prison camps."

Before Johnny could comment, the ward doors flew open and half a dozen Japanese soldiers burst in, shouting and gesticulating at the prisoners. They started jabbing at the helpless men with their bayonets, giving Johnny a demonstration of what his soldier-ghost had been trying to explain.

Then, in keeping with the endless surprises his nightly journeys had been providing, Johnny witnessed another act of unbelievable courage. The nurses all rushed down to where the patients were lying. Pushing the soldiers aside, they formed a ring around the men in the beds. There they stood, silently defying the armed Japanese. The minutes ticked by, during which the soldiers waved their weapons menacingly at the nurses. But the women never wavered. Eventually, the soldiers gave up and left the ward, shouting threats and insults.

Johnny looked dumbstruck at his soldier-ghost, who echoed the boy's thoughts. "It takes a special kind of courage to do something like that, doesn't it? And what makes it more remarkable is that it happens at some time or other virtually every day. And every time the nurses defy the soldiers until they leave."

"If it wasn't for this hospital and the nurses, I guess a lot of these soldiers would die?"

"No doubt about it. Unfortunately, as I explained, it isn't going to last much longer. Soon, they will all be shipped to prison camps. Well, that's not quite accurate. The doctors and the patients will be sent to camps, but the nurses' fate will be different. You see, the Japanese never knew what to do with the women — and the children, for that matter — they captured. In their eyes they were just a problem they would rather not deal with. So what they will do with the nurses is what they have done with all the other women they captured: keep shunting them from one camp to another.

"The result of this policy means most of them spend weeks and months simply walking from place to place, with many of the women dying of exhaustion and lack of food. Maybe that is the idea."

Johnny looked shocked at this callousness. Seeing the

look, the soldier-ghost spoke again. "Remember what I said before about there being no such thing as a nice war? This is another example of how it desensitizes human beings. War creates many great heroes, but never confuse that with the idea that war itself is heroic. It can be both tragic and brutal. At times, though this may surprise you, it can even be farcical. But never is war itself heroic."

Johnny stood silent, once again unable to find any response to everything he had heard and seen. Eventually, trying to get his mind off it all, he asked about the man they had come to see, whom so far Johnny had not been able to find among the patients.

"Geoff Marston's in that bed. He is the one speaking to the nurse." Johnny's soldier-ghost pointed across the ward. The man bore no resemblance to the filthy prisoner with the matted hair and beard he had seen staggering into the place that passed for a hospital in North Point Camp.

"He looks so different."

"Oh yes. Considering their very limited resources, the staff here are performing miracles."

"What happens to the prisoners when they recover?"

"Whether they recover or not, they will all soon be sent to prison camps. Some who have virtually recovered, like Geoff Marston, will go very soon. What he's trying to do before then is find out what happened to the two Canadian women, nurses who came out with the battalion."

"Canadian *women* went to war back then?"

"Not in the way they do today. They were never allowed to fly fighters or bombers or drive tanks. They did, in fact, fly planes, but only as ferry pilots, taking the planes to where they were needed.

"You see, various governments in this war have an ambiguous attitude about sending women into war zones. Although they refuse to let the servicewomen go overseas, for some odd reason they haven't applied the ban to nurses. I guess their thinking is the enemy won't harm nurses. But what happened to some of them here when the Japanese entered the city shows how wrong they were."

"What happened?"

"Many of them suffered horribly at the hands of drunken soldiers. They were raped, beaten. Fortunately, the two Canadians weren't physically harmed. But Kay Christie, that's the name of the one from Toronto, formed a close friendship with an English nurse who was one of the unlucky ones. Kay will have nightmares for years over what happened to her friend.

"But to return to your question, nurses actually served in many war zones, as you will see during our trips. Another aspect of this strange way of using women is that the British government itself showed little compunction about sending them into occupied countries as spies. Many will lose their lives while others will be captured and tortured. It is a tribute to their courage that the enemy will get little information from any of them. We will see more of this kind of courage from women, because it's important you understand as much as possible about all Canadians who took part in this war."

Johnny was silent for a moment, trying to take everything in so he could tell it all to Casey. Finally he spoke. "What's the other Canadian nurse's name?"

"May Walters. She is from Winnipeg."

"And will Geoff Marston get to see the two of them?"

"Let's listen in and find out." A touch of his soldier-ghost's hand and they were standing by Geoff Marston's bed.

The nurse was speaking. "They are safe and well but I'm afraid you won't be able to see them. They are in another section of the hospital, and none of the nurses or patients is allowed to go from one to the other. Perhaps the Japs think we'll get together and revolt." She said this with a bitter laugh.

Johnny remembered what his soldier-ghost had said about the hospital closing and the nurses, along with other women and children, having to walk from one camp to another.

"Will the two Canadian nurses survive?"

"Oh yes. In fact they will get lucky. They will spend more than a year on the road or staying in dilapidated old camps with few facilities. Then one morning they will be ordered to stay behind while the others are sent on the road again. They will think they are about to experience what their friends suffered when Hong Kong first fell. But instead they will be loaded into a truck and driven to an airfield. To their astonishment, they will be put on a plane with a load of

American women, both nurses and civilians, and flown to the States. On the journey they will discover that the Americans have done a prisoner swap with the Japanese to get their women released, and have agreed to take the Canadians as well. So Kay and May will return safely home."

"Why did the Japanese do that?"

"Remember what I said about them wanting to get rid of the women prisoners because they didn't know what to do with them? Well, I guess this was their chance to get rid of a couple more. Unfortunately, for the British women, their government had nothing to trade. Come, time's up."

Chapter 11

JOHNNY WAS BOTH impatient and apprehensive about meeting Casey at school the next day: he was keen to tell Casey about his latest adventure, but wasn't sure how she'd feel about having dinner with his parents. He didn't get the ·chance to talk to her at the lunch break. But when he finally met her after school and timidly mentioned the invitation, he was relieved to hear her laugh.

"Hey, don't sweat it. I'm sure I'll survive."

Johnny's sigh of relief was almost as audible as Casey's laugh.

"So, now tell me about last night," she whispered conspiratorially.

Casey's flippant attitude disappeared as Johnny told her

the story of Bill Chong's brush with death, astonishing escape, and of the nurses' defiance of the Japanese soldiers.

Hey eyes were full of admiration as Johnny came to the end of his adventures from the night before. "Gosh, can you imagine going through that? I never heard of Canadian women really being in the war. I mean, I knew they joined the forces, and there were many that were nurses. But I never heard of them actually being in a war zone, did you?"

Johnny shook his head, not wanting to admit that it had never even occurred to him until last night that there had been *any* women in the war.

"Did you get into the book before you went to bed?"

"Yeah, and from what I read about your great-grandfather's battles in Russia, all of those people who fought in those wars were something special."

"Let's get home, and then you can fill me in on how far you got with the book."

As they walked toward Casey's house, Johnny brought up something else that had been on his mind. "You seem so cool with all this. Don't you find it freaky?"

"Weird, bizarre, freaky, all of the above. But we just have to wait and see what it all means. I have no doubt that we'll find out."

—◦◦◦—

"So?" Casey and Johnny were in her room, Casey sprawled on the bed, Johnny on her computer chair. "Tell me what you thought about the book."

"I was really amazed at the problems your great-grand-father had just getting supplies for his squadron. You'd think the Russians would want to do all they could to help."

"And how about the ones they sent to be trained as pilots? Seems all they did was get drunk and fight. No wonder they lost."

"And can you imagine having to fly those planes in that kind of weather?" Johnny shuddered, thinking about the ride he had taken on Raymond Collishaw's plane and what it would be like to fly one in the middle of a Russian winter.

"What about the guys who had to look after them?"

"Yeah, I guess they all had to be pretty tough."

"Did you get to the part about my great-grandfather getting typhoid? Where he almost died but was saved by a Russian countess? Wasn't that romantic — her taking him home and nursing him?"

Johnny was taken aback. The thought that Casey was the least bit romantic, like other girls, had simply never entered his head. Most times he never even thought of her as a girl. In Johnny's mind she was, simply, his best friend. In fact, she was his only friend.

"Well, yeah, I guess it was," he stammered in reply.

"I thought it was really tragic when he went back to the village to try and find her and she was gone."

"I never got that far. What happened to her?"

"He never found out. But it seems that the village was probably raided by the Communist armies. And I guess she would have been arrested, being a part of the old regime they were fighting."

"Do you think she survived?"

"Probably not. After all, if they could execute the Czar and all his family, I doubt they would worry too much about shooting a countess."

"I'm sure glad we don't do things like that here." Johnny shuddered at the thought of growing up in such a place.

"Yeah, I guess we are really lucky to live where we do. Anyway, you still have a lot of reading to do, so you should get home and get at it. I'll see you tomorrow at your house."

"OK."

The realization that Casey was coming to supper the next day gave Johnny plenty to brood about on his way home. He wondered what his parents would think of Casey and her grungy clothes.

Once he got home and had his supper, Johnny again became engrossed in the book, and read non-stop until bedtime.

Curling up under his duvet, he mused that he would have a lot to talk about with Casey the next day. He fell asleep wondering where his soldier-ghost would take him this time.

—⁓—

Johnny found himself high up in some mountains. He noticed an old stone farmhouse at the back of a ploughed, stony field. From somewhere below came a constant barrage of artillery, the shells screaming over the farmhouse and exploding about half a mile away at an unseen target. Some of the shells exploded in the air, sending shrapnel to the ground below.

"Where are we now?"

"Northern Italy. Winston Churchill, the prime minister of Great Britain, has insisted the Allied armies make their first invasion of Hitler's European stronghold from what he calls its 'soft underbelly' — not that it is proving very soft. Hitler has sent one of his best field commanders, a man named Kesselring, to defend Germany's back door. He is fighting a very clever and stubborn rearguard, which is giving the Allies a lot of trouble."

"So did Churchill make a mistake?"

"Well, not necessarily, although it is probably the one decision Churchill makes that stems too much from his own personal feelings, rather than from his usual cold, hard, practical approach."

"How so?"

"In the First World War, it was Churchill who authorized the invasion of Turkey from the sea. It was a huge failure, with most of the soldiers, many of whom were Australian, getting killed. Ever since, Churchill has had a fear of any sea-born invasion. It is for that reason he has insisted on invading via Italy first, because he feels it would prove easier and give the Allies more experience before the main invasion of France, which is still to come."

Just at that moment, the door of the farmhouse was flung open and a man dressed in a farmer's smock with a battered old felt hat jammed on his head stormed out carrying a hoe, which he brandished in the direction from where the shells were coming. Shouting curses, the man began walking among the ploughed rows in the field, jabbing away at the stony soil while the shells continued to scream over his head.

Johnny couldn't believe his eyes. "He's hoeing his field."

The soldier-ghost chuckled. "Not really. He's just pretending, so that he can find the break in his transmission wire. You see, he is an Allied soldier, and it is he who is directing the artillery fire at the German soldiers, who are dug in over there. They have four tanks that are pinning down the Allied soldiers, and they have to be destroyed."

Johnny's eyes opened even wider than before. "But the Germans can only be maybe a kilometre away. Isn't he afraid of being shot?"

"Well, actually, I misled you a bit there. He is more than just a soldier. He is from a special commando unit, and he is why we are here."

"He's Canadian then?"

"Yes. More specifically, he is a Saulteaux Indian from Manitoba named Tommy Prince and he is a sergeant-major in probably the most unusual fighting unit among the Allies."

"Unusual? How?"

"It is known as the First Special Services Force, although it has already earned the nickname of the 'Black Devils' from the Germans, the 'black' part referring to their practice of blacking their faces with boot polish for night action. The unit is made up of both Canadian and American soldiers, and they are all trained in mountain warfare. What makes them unusual is that they are commanded by both Canadian and American officers. You'd have to go back a long way in history to find the last time any sovereign nation has allowed its troops to come directly under the command of foreign officers in battle. Even when they do form part of a larger military force, with an overall commander from another country, the troops themselves still take their orders from their own officers in the field, and are led into battle by them. In the case of the Black Devils, they all functioned as one unit. They even wore identical uniforms while on missions."

"So, this Tommy Prince is a Canadian hero?"

"Both a hero and a tragic figure."

Johnny was intrigued. "How so?"

"Tommy will become one of the most decorated natives to serve in this war. His actions here will earn him the Military Medal from the British. Later he will be awarded the Silver Star by the Americans. When this war is over, he will go on to serve in Korea, a conflict that will follow very soon after the end of this one. In Korea, Tommy will be wounded and invalided out of the army, and that's where the tragic part comes in."

"Why?"

"Because soldiering is all Tommy knows. It's what makes him feel equal to the white man in a time when natives, like the Chinese, are not treated as equals. Once he loses that, he will degenerate into heavy drinking, sometimes selling his medals to buy liquor, then pretending they were stolen to get another set, until the drinking eventually kills him."

By this time, Tommy Prince had reached the end of the field, stopping along the way to shake his fist alternately at the German positions and at where the Allied gunfire was coming from.

Suddenly he bent down, and after a short period straightened up with a handful of rocks, which he threw disgustedly to the side of the field. He then turned, and with more fist-shaking, made his way back to the farmhouse, slamming the door behind him.

The soldier-ghost chuckled. "He found the break and fixed it. Come, it's time for us to move on."

"What did he get the American Silver Star for?"

"Good question — let's find out."

With the familiar touch, Johnny found himself in another mountainous region.

"We are in the mountains of southern France, which the Allies have also invaded, to put pressure on Hitler's European fortress from all sides. But they have reached an impasse. They know there is a reserve battalion of Germans well dug in near a place called L'Escarène, and it would be too risky to attack without knowing exactly where they are so that they can be neutralized. It has been decided that someone has to infiltrate enemy lines to assess their strength and locate roads and bridges in the area."

"And Tommy's going to do it?"

"You're getting quicker on the uptake. Let's follow them."

"Them?"

"Yes, Tommy is taking one private with him."

They moved again, and Johnny found himself standing on an outcrop of rock that looked down on a mountain meadow. There was no sign of the two men.

"Where are they?"

"The private is tucked into a small cleft below us, covering Tommy's back. Tommy is somewhere down there working his way toward the German lines, which are on the other side of the meadow in those mountains." The soldier-ghost pointed to where the mountains rose again on the other side of the meadow.

"It's too dark to see him."

Johnny's soldier-ghost smiled. "It wouldn't make any difference if it was daylight. You still wouldn't see him. That's why he's been chosen."

After watching for a while, Johnny's soldier-ghost spoke. "He's back." He pointed to where he had said Tommy's backup was hiding. Suddenly, two figures appeared out of the darkness and moved toward them.

"I didn't see anything." Johnny looked stunned.

His soldier-ghost smiled again. "What you saw was a First Nations warrior doing something he is a master at."

At that moment, from somewhere behind them, firing broke out.

Immediately Tommy Prince and the private went into a crouching run, heading toward the shooting.

Johnny's soldier-ghost touched his hand and they were standing on a cliff. Below them Johnny could see German soldiers crouched behind rocks firing at a small group of men in civilian clothes.

"They are French Resistance fighters. They look to be in a bit of trouble. They must be outnumbered about two to one, but I suspect they are about to receive some unexpected help." He pointed to where Tommy Prince and the private were crouched behind a rock outcropping.

A continuous hail of fire came pouring out from where the two men were, throwing the German soldiers into total confusion. Many of them fell before they even realized where the new threat was coming from. In a matter of minutes, the remaining Germans took off scrambling for the safety of the mountains.

The French Resistance fighters slowly came out from their cover and looked up. Tommy Prince left his spot and moved toward them, followed by the private.

One of the Frenchman called to Tommy, "Where's the rest of your company?"

Tommy grinned and jerked his thumb at the private coming down behind him.

"*Mon Dieu.* There are only two of you. I thought you had a whole company up there."

Johnny's soldier-ghost spoke again. "Tommy would have

had yet another medal for this, except for an unfortunate incident."

"What happens?"

"A dispatch will be sent to French H.Q. recommending him for France's Croix de Guerre. But the dispatcher will be killed and the recommendation never received. But he is going to get his Silver Star for this patrol because the information he brings back will enable the Americans to pinpoint the German reserve battalion, neutralize them and successfully drive them out of the area."

"What about Canada? They must have decorated him, or at least remembered what he did?"

"That's another real tragedy of war. Once it's over, people quickly forget those that come back. I suppose it's understandable in a way. They just want to return to some sense of normalcy and forget the tragedies and suffering. But that doesn't excuse governments, who could do a better job of recognizing the sacrifices of these men and women."

"So, he gets forgotten then?"

"Not quite. An attempt is finally made. If you go to Winnipeg, you will find a street named after him."

"Well, that's something, isn't it?" Johnny said, seeing the unhappy look on his soldier-ghost's face.

"Something, yes. The only trouble with this kind of recognition is that unless someone already knows who the person was and what he or she did, it's meaningless. There is a boulevard in Calgary named after a Canadian who was the top fighter ace during the first year of this war, yet few local people know who he was. Politicians love the idea of commemorating war heroes this way, though. It's cheap."

The sarcasm was not lost on Johnny.

Chapter 12

JOHNNY AWOKE BUT did not move for a while, thinking partly about his adventures of the night before, but also about the fact that it was Saturday, and Casey was coming to supper. He lay wondering, as he had since his mother had insisted on inviting her over, what his parents' reaction to her would be.

He finally stirred and jumped out of bed as his mother's voice reached him from the kitchen. "Johnny, are you dressed yet? Your breakfast is almost ready."

"I'm up, Mom." With that, he rushed into the bathroom and, throwing off his pajamas, leaped into the shower.

"That was quick. I hope you showered properly." Mrs. Anders turned from the stove as her son jumped the last four stairs and appeared in the kitchen. She placed Johnny's breakfast in front of him, peering at him closely as if trying to verify his cleanliness. Johnny had barely spooned in the first mouthful when his mother asked, "Did you remind Casey about tonight?"

"Yes, Mom. She'll be here."

"Good. We are so looking forward to meeting her. Are you seeing her today?"

"This morning."

"Where are you meeting?"

"Just in the park, Mom."

A look of approval appeared on his mother's face. "Well, you can give her a little reminder this morning then, just to be sure."

"Mom, she won't forget," Johnny replied, wishing his mother wouldn't keep harping on about the visit.

"Give it a rest, dear," his father put in.

"Thanks, Dad," Johnny muttered under his breath.

Mrs. Anders sniffed. "A little reminder is always a good idea. After all, Johnny would forget which day of the week it was without being reminded."

"Casey's nothing like that, Mom. She's really organized." As soon as the words came out, Johnny regretted them, well aware that Casey would not fit his mother's idea of being organized.

"If you say so. Now eat your breakfast. It's getting cold," his mother finished up, as if it were Johnny's fault he hadn't been eating.

As soon as he had finished his breakfast, Johnny grabbed his coat and took off before his mother had the chance to give him yet another reminder.

———

"So, how did it go last night?"

Casey and Johnny were strolling through the park, kicking dead leaves and watching them swirl and scatter in the blustery wind.

Johnny immediately forgot about his mother and launched into an animated account of his wanderings with his soldier-ghost. When he finished, he glanced at Casey and realized she was looking at him with a mixture of admiration and envy.

"So, Johnny Anders, while I was sleeping the night away with boring old regular dreams, you were wandering around the Italian and French Alps, watching this Tommy Prince being a hero. So lucky!"

Johnny was taken aback by the envy in Casey's voice. "Oh jeez, I'm sorry, I never thought about that."

"Don't be lame. I'm not upset. But who wouldn't be envious? You get to see history in the making. And you get to see what war is really like, and what those people went through."

Johnny relaxed. "I never looked at it like that. I am so freaking dumb sometimes."

"It may have escaped your notice, Johnny Anders, but I don't do 'dumb,' so don't tick me off by suggesting I'd waste my time with someone dumb." Casey's smile took every bit of the sting from her words.

Johnny nodded in agreement, still marvelling at his luck that she had been in the library that day.

Casey looked at her watch. "Hey, I've got to go. Otherwise my mom will lose it. See you tonight." With a wave, Casey took off at a run, leaving Johnny waving at her departing back, his own, "Yeah, see you," whipped away by the wind.

Chapter 13

JOHNNY HAD BEEN fidgeting in the kitchen all afternoon until finally his mother said with exasperation, "Johnny, for goodness' sake, go and find something to do. Go and read your book or something. I'm trying to make supper and you're driving me crazy."

Johnny went to his bedroom and picked up Raymond Collishaw's book. But he couldn't concentrate, his mind on Casey's visit and how his parents would react to her. One thing he was sure of: whatever image they might have formed of his new friend, Casey, with her tattered old clothes, would not be it. For a moment he found himself wishing Casey were a punk. Even though his mother wouldn't exactly be excited, at least she knew what a punk looked like. Then he shook off the thought. He felt enormous relief when his watch finally ticked around to four-thirty. At least now he could occupy himself with getting ready.

At five o'clock on the nose, he parked himself close to the window, where he would be able to see Casey arriving. At five-fifteen, a car appeared around the corner. Without waiting for it to stop, Johnny shot into the hall and stood by the front door.

When the bell rang, he took a deep breath and pulled the door open. Then his mouth did a perfect imitation of what it had done when Casey's mother told him their family name.

The Casey he knew had vanished completely. Standing in her place was a girl dressed in brand-new jeans and sneakers. The jeans were topped by a crisp white blouse over which she wore a short, fitted red jacket that complemented her auburn hair, which was swept back over her ears to end in a long ponytail.

"May I come in? It's cold." Casey, fully aware of the effect she was having on Johnny, smiled sweetly.

Johnny still couldn't speak, mesmerized by her Cinderella-like transformation.

"Johnny, are you going to let Casey in, or are you going to keep her on the doorstep all night?"

His mother's voice finally shook him out of his daze. "Yes, Mom, of course."

He swung the door wide, giving his mother, who had appeared from the kitchen, her first look at Casey. His trepidation about the evening melted away.

"You never told us she was pretty as well as clever, Johnny." The beaming smile on his mother's face told Johnny that everything was going to be OK.

As they entered the living room, Johnny's father put down his paper and rose to greet Casey, his eyebrows arching upward as he caught sight of her. Then he turned to his son. "Now I can see what spurred this sudden interest in history."

Johnny was by now relaxed enough to allow a small smile at his father's words. But he couldn't help wondering what his father would say if he saw the other Casey, and if he knew the real reason behind his interest in history.

"Come, everyone," his mother called. "Supper is ready and I don't want it getting cold. Casey, you sit here next to me, so we can chat."

The meal went off like a dream, with Johnny contributing little, content to observe Casey working her charm on his parents.

After supper, they took off for his room, Casey being careful to ask permission of Johnny's parents first, and receiving a further look of approval in the process.

"Well, did I pass?"

"Pass? Are you kidding? I've never seen my parents so impressed. How do you do it? I sure couldn't."

"Yes, you could. Should we have a look at the book?"

Emboldened by how well things had gone, Johnny decided to take the plunge and ask Casey the question that had been bugging him ever since he opened the front door.

"Why don't you dress like that more often? I mean . . ." Johnny started to stumble, but was determined not to give up. "You look so . . . I mean, any of the guys . . ."

Casey cut Johnny short, a frown on her face. "That's exactly why. I'm no one's trophy to be shown off, and I won't become one just to please some macho jerk who needs a boost to his ego. They can all take a hike if that's all they're looking for."

Johnny was surprised by the intensity of Casey's words. "Jeez, Casey, I never meant it that way. It's just that I, you know, kinda wondered, that's all."

Her smile returned. "Do you think I don't know that, idiot? Even your magic stories wouldn't be enough to keep you around if I thought you were like that. But I already figured out that's not your thing, and I figure you don't need me freaking your parents out."

"Wow, you didn't have to do that for me," Johnny blurted out.

"Oh, so now you're telling me you don't like my new look and you wouldn't enjoy, just a little, showing me off. Now I'm devastated."

Johnny was about to protest when he saw her mischievous smile. "Well, who wouldn't? I mean you really are . . . like . . . well . . . you know."

Casey laughed delightedly. "I think somewhere in all that was a compliment. At least, I'll take it as one.

"Anyway, I have an idea that will finally prove to us that

you really are being shown the past." Casey walked over to Johnny's computer and switched it on. "I bet we can find the story of this Tommy Prince on the Department of Veteran Affairs website."

Johnny banged his head. "Jeez, why didn't I think about that before?"

"It wouldn't have helped before. I already checked and I couldn't find anything on Bill Chong or Geoff Marston. But maybe it's because one was a civilian and the other was a prisoner of war. Hey, here we go — Tommy Prince."

Johnny leaned over Casey's shoulder and read the summary on Tommy Prince. It was exactly as his soldier-ghost had told him.

"So there. So long as you didn't look this all up online before as part of some weird plan to trick me, then this shows that your soldier-ghost is real." Casey giggled at her own words. "I can't believe I just said that. How can a ghost be real? I think this ghost of yours is making me crazy, too."

Johnny didn't respond at first. He was still absorbing the fact that although Casey had seemed to accept his story of the ghost, she had obviously still had doubts. So much so, that she had attempted to check out the Chong and Marston stories.

"I swear I didn't know anything about any of this war stuff until the soldier-ghost came along."

"OK. I believe you. Now let's get on with your essay. Where are you at in the book?"

Johnny shook his head, thinking, *Well, wouldn't you be suspicious if someone told you such an insane story?* He put his hurt feelings aside and smiled. "I've just started reading the part about when they had to retreat across Russia on that old wreck of a train."

"Oh yeah, that's a really good part. Didn't that trip sound horrendous? Makes me feel like a jerk for complaining so much about road trips with my parents."

"I really want to do this essay right, Casey. It's kind of important for us to know about our past, isn't it?"

"That's another reason I like you, Johnny Anders. You care about things. Of course it's important."

"I didn't used to. And if it wasn't for these weird visits from this ghost, which I still don't get, and meeting you, I never would."

"I don't believe that for a minute. As for your ghost, I don't understand it either. All I know is what you're seeing really did happen. Are you making lots of notes for your essay?"

"I've got a notebook full already. I hope I can understand it all and make it work."

"Good, then show me what you've got."

For the rest of the evening, Casey watched Johnny work and rework his notes, speaking only to comment on his ideas for the essay.

Not until Mrs. Anders called, "Casey, your mother's here for you," did either of them look up from their work.

Casey rose and stretched, followed by Johnny who, while carefully placing his sheaf of notes on his desk, was wondering, not for the first time, how he had got so lucky.

Mrs. Collishaw was chatting with Johnny's parents when they reached the living room. She turned to smile at her daughter. "Ready, dear?"

"Yes, Mom." Casey turned to Johnny's parents and thanked them for the lovely time, a comment that brought smiles to the faces of both her mother and Johnny, but for entirely different reasons.

At the door, she gave Johnny a quick squeeze on the arm and a look that capped a perfect evening for him.

"Well, I don't know what I was expecting Casey to be like, but I certainly never expected her to be so smart, charming and well-mannered, Johnny." His mother was looking at her son with a mixture of delight and surprise.

"Yes, how did you do it? The other boys must be green with envy," his father chimed in.

Johnny could barely suppress a smile at the thought of what his parents would have said if Casey had turned up in her usual throwaway outfit. He came close to bursting out laughing, his face reddening with the effort.

"I think we are embarrassing the boy, dear," his mother said, misunderstanding Johnny's red face, but, thankfully, letting him off the hook.

Johnny's father laughed. "OK, off you go."

Johnny shot off up to his room, calling back, "Night, Mom. Night, Dad."

Chapter 14

JASON LEE WAS AT the front of the group of staring boys and girls as Johnny strolled into the schoolyard holding Casey's hand. Casey, dressed in an outfit similar to the one she had worn the previous day, smiled at the boys as they approached.

"I don't believe it. How did Anders get someone like that?" Jason yelled.

"Yeah, and who is she?" someone else asked.

"Well, let's see if we can give the lovebirds a scare." Eddie Roy, a known bully, tossed a firecracker at Casey's feet. The firecracker exploded, sending a cloud of acrid smoke into their faces. Johnny charged toward the laughing crowd —

and promptly fell out of bed and onto the floor.

"Whoa, steady there, boy. We have a lot to see yet. Don't go breaking your leg." Johnny looked up from the floor at his soldier-ghost, who was regarding him with amusement, his hand outstretched. Feeling foolish, Johnny scrambled to his feet and took his soldier-ghost's hand. He was immediately transported to a place where brilliant sunshine sparkled off blue water.

"We are in Cypress, on the Mediterranean coast of Europe," the soldier-ghost said, and Johnny understood why the water was so blue and the weather so hot. "And those are Allied ships in the harbour."

Johnny looked around at the beautiful old town and noticed five nurses disembarking from a small boat.

"They are from that ship out there," the soldier-ghost said, pointing to a ship moored alongside another about half a mile offshore. "It is a hospital ship called the *Lady Nelson*, which is here to collect wounded servicemen and take them back to Britain."

"Is that why we're here?"

"That's right. Remember the nurses in Hong Kong? I said we would see more of the paradox that banned women from combat, yet happily sent them into danger as nurses and spies. Well, this is another example of the risks they took. That ship will — as it has done over and over — sail for Britain in a convoy tomorrow. It will sail the Mediterranean, where it is vulnerable to enemy air attacks, then into the

Atlantic, where German U-boats are always lurking. In fact, the *Lady Nelson* herself has already been sunk once. But, fortunately, not as a hospital ship. Oddly, she was sunk right here, in the Mediterranean. Then she was raised and refitted as a hospital ship, to become the first Canadian hospital ship of the war."

"Wow. But they wouldn't attack it now that it's a hospital ship, would they?" asked Johnny, pointing to the mammoth red cross painted on the side of the *Lady Nelson*.

"*She*, not *it*. All ships at this time are called 'she.' To answer your question, the Geneva Convention, which lays down certain rules of engagement in war, and which all these countries have signed, says no. But apart from the obvious fact that mistakes occur every day in war, our friend Mr. Hitler has spent the last ten years producing a particularly nasty breed of military people. So while most Germans respect the convention, some of these nasty types can be found in all branches of his military."

"Are these nurses Canadian then?" asked Johnny, as the five women started walking toward the harbour town.

"Oh yes," the soldier-ghost said. "There are seven more on the ship, in addition to their matron, a real old disciplinarian from Montreal named Charlotte Nixon, who served as a nurse in the First World War. There are also six doctors on board."

The group of women headed to a sidewalk café, where they sat down at an outside table and ordered refreshments.

But they were never given the chance to taste their drinks, because just as the waiter left with their order, a huge explosion erupted in the harbour, shattering windows and blowing off the roofs of buildings close to the water.

Everyone, including the nurses, rushed to where they could get a better look at what had happened, all pointing at a rising plume of smoke.

"My God, that's our ship," one of them burst out, and they all broke into a run back to the harbour and the tender that had brought them ashore. The officer and his crew were standing by the boat, peering out over the water as the smoke billowed upward.

The officer, hearing the commotion behind him, turned and saw the nurses. "I'm sorry, ladies, but it looks as if the ship you tied up alongside was an ammo ship, and it just exploded, setting your ship on fire."

"Then we must get back," they all chorused, heading for the moored tender. "Some of our people are still on board."

"Absolutely not, ladies. I can't take you out there. It's far too dangerous."

"But you must, Lieutenant. We are needed."

The officer stood firm. "I'm sorry, ladies. I can't take you. My commanding officer would court martial me for putting you and my crew in danger." With that he turned away, indicating the conversation was over.

The five nurses also turned away, realizing the officer wasn't going to budge.

"What are we going to do?" one of them said. "We have to get back on board."

"What about him?" One of the nurses, who had been glancing around the docks, spoke up, pointing to a boyish-looking American officer. Like his British counterpart, he was standing near a moored tender, gazing out at the fire raging on the water.

The other four needed no urging, and they all converged on the American. But before they could reach him, he turned and went into a small hut a short distance away.

Undeterred, the nurses barged into the hut. With a touch of his soldier-ghost's hand, Johnny found himself inside, too. The American, who had just sat down behind a desk, looked up in surprise.

"What can I do for you ladies?" He smiled, showing a row of perfect white teeth.

"You can get us back to our ship."

"You mean that hospital ship? Are you crazy? That thing could blow up any second."

"But we have to. They need us out there."

"But ladies, I can't. It's just too damn dangerous. Excuse my language."

However, the nurses sensed he had a soft spot for women, so a couple of them perched themselves on the corners of his desk and began flirting with him. The lieutenant didn't stand a chance. His last ounce of resistance collapsed when the other three began to cry.

"OK, OK, I'll take you out. But I'm not going on board. Once you are on board, you're on your own."

The two sitting on the desk leaned over and kissed the blushing American on the cheeks while the others dried their tears. "Thank you, Lieutenant. You're very kind," they all chorused.

Before he could change his mind, he was hustled out of the hut and onto his tender, the nurses piling in after him.

His crew stared, mouths agape, when he gave his order. "Come on, men, we have to get these nurses back to their ship. They are desperately needed."

"That one, sir?" asked a seaman with stripes on his arm, suggesting that he was the senior crew member. "Jeez, that thing's sitting next to a time bomb."

"Come on, Murphy. We are only going to pull alongside. The nurses will climb onto the ship themselves. We'll only be there a few minutes."

"In this crazy war, it only takes a few minutes to die," the man grumbled, but waved his crew on board. They cast off as the officer started the engines.

It was only when the officer brought his tender alongside the *Lady Nelson*, on the opposite side of where the ammunition ship was still smouldering, that the nurses fully realized what they had let themselves in for. The regular gangway was also on the far side, and the only access from this side to the deck, far above, was a pair of rope ladders swinging in the breeze.

But there was no going back now. Taking a deep breath, the first two grabbed a ladder each and started the climb, followed by the next pair. With their skirts billowing in the wind, none of the nurses even dared think what the American sailors in the tender were seeing as they held the rope ladders.

Finally, they all scrambled over the rail, tumbling onto the deck. With a wave, the Americans let go of the rope ladders, and the tender pulled away, taking with it any hope of going back.

"Get up, nurses, and tidy yourselves. You look disgraceful." The nurses climbed to their feet, smoothing down their skirts as they looked into the face of their matron, staring at them as if they had just fallen from the sky.

"How did you get here?"

"We persuaded an American tender to bring us out, matron, so that we could help."

"And how did you get up on deck?"

"We climbed up using the rope ladders, matron."

Matron Nixon walked over to the side of the ship and gazed down at the rope ladders, swaying back and forth. She sniffed loudly. "Well, now that you've all made a complete exhibition of yourselves, I'd better see some real effort at redemption. Get yourselves into the wards. We have a lot to do before we sail in the morning."

"Yes, matron," the nurses replied, barely hiding the grins on their faces as they ran toward the ship's wards.

As they disappeared, a smile drifted across Matron Nixon's own face before she followed the nurses. Johnny, who had watched the whole scene unfold in mesmerized silence, finally spoke. "Are they going to be all right?"

"Oh yes. If you look over at the other side of the ship, you will see that a harbour fire tender has put out the fire on the ammo ship. The *Lady Nelson* was never actually on fire herself. It just appeared that way to the people standing on the shore. The hardest job is going to be the clean-up of the *Lady Nelson*, because virtually everything is covered with soot."

"But the matron said they have to sail in the morning. Don't all the injured people still have to be brought on board?"

"Five hundred to be exact, which helps explain why I am showing you this. None of these people will close their eyes tonight, and those nurses will work their hearts out, scrubbing and cleaning the wards. Those wounded soldiers will get on board on time, and the *Lady Nelson* will sail on time for England. Unfortunately, we can't wait for that because I have one more incident regarding a Canadian nurse I want you to see before the night has passed. Come."

Johnny felt the touch of his soldier-ghost's hand and suddenly they were standing in dense jungle. It was so reminiscent of the jungles of China where he had seen Bill Chong that he thought that they were there. But then Johnny saw the prison camp, with its gates wide open and a group of

Japanese soldiers lounging around the gate. His soldier-ghost explained that they were in Indonesia.

Just at that moment, a Jeep came into the camp and skidded to a halt. A lone woman climbed out. The woman was stocky, with a no-nonsense look about her. She was wearing a uniform with the letters FANY on each shoulder.

"Lieutenant Joan Bamford Fletcher, a member of the First Aid Nursing Yeomanry, who hails from Regina," explained the soldier-ghost.

Johnny was baffled. "But there are Japanese soldiers standing there. Isn't this a pretty dangerous thing to do?"

"It might have been dangerous a short while ago, but it is 1945 now and the Japanese have just surrendered."

"But why is she here on her own? Where are our soldiers?"

"Two hundred and eighty miles away, in Padang. She has been sent here by a naïve British officer to bring these Allied prisoners from this camp, at Bankinang, in northern Sumatra, to Padang, where they can receive medical attention and eventually be taken home. The Allies have little knowledge of Sumatra, and the officer must have thought Bankinang was just up the road."

"But how can she do it on her own?"

"That's what she is trying to figure out. Let's watch and see."

Joan Bamford Fletcher was indeed trying to figure out how she was going to transport a load of very sick prisoners on a journey that, as she had already discovered, had to pass through the Indonesian jungles, which were full of hostile rebels.

Her eyes swept the area. She noticed that the Japanese soldiers had a fleet of trucks standing at the perimeter of the clearing surrounding the prison camp. Next, her eyes took in the soldiers standing there watching her, their expressions as puzzled as Johnny's.

Joan realized there was only one solution. She gestured to a Japanese officer to come over.

"Do you speak any English?"

To her surprise and relief, he answered in perfect English. "Yes. I studied in America for three years."

"Good. Listen. I have been sent here to bring these people to Padang. How many are there?"

"About seventeen hundred."

"My God. Where are they all?"

"We confined them to their huts until we received orders." The officer pointed at the far side of the compound where Joan could just see some huts, half hidden in the trees of the jungle.

"Right, well, it's pretty obvious that you must be the only fit men around, and you have the transport. So I want fifteen of those trucks and enough of your men to man them. The others are to remain here and look after the rest until we return for them. Understood?"

The man bowed. "Perfectly," he said. He then barked an

order in Japanese and some of the men immediately rushed over to the trucks, selecting fifteen that had machine guns mounted on them. These were started and driven through the camp gate.

Within an hour, the soldiers had loaded the trucks with the sickest prisoners and they were on their way. Johnny and his soldier-ghost rode in the lead truck with Bamford-Fletcher.

At first, the Indonesian rebels kept their distance when they saw the machine guns and Japanese soldiers. But as the journey progressed, they became bolder, dancing in front of the lead truck until the last moment, when they would finally jump aside. The convoy was particularly vulnerable when it was forced to stop. Then the rebels began dragging fallen trees, or whatever else they could find, into the road to make the convey halt, so they could attack it.

But to Joan's surprise, the Japanese soldiers justified her faith in them by fighting off the rebels with fierce determination.

Watching all this, Johnny exclaimed, "I don't think I would ever have believed this if I'd only read about it."

"That's why I wanted you to see it. The war might be over, but what this woman is doing deserves a medal. Fortunately, she will get one, as well as a dose of swamp fever to go with it. But we must now take another jump forward, because we don't have time to follow them all the way." A touch of the hand and they were standing in the main street of Padang, where the convoy was just arriving after fourteen nerve-racking hours on the road.

Its arrival caused a sensation. British soldiers, on seeing the armed Japanese, immediately raised their rifles and aimed them squarely at the convoy. But then Joan Bamford Fletcher popped her head out of the lead truck, identified herself and explained.

The soldiers' suspicion turned to disbelief as they grasped the fact of what she had done. Once it sank in, they started to cheer and wave at the strange convoy as it proceeded to the military hospital.

After all her charges were safely in the hospital, Joan reported to the British officer who had sent her on the mission.

"Two hundred and eighty miles. I had no idea. You should have returned for help," the stunned officer said.

"I found some very good help, thank you."

"Well, yes, but now you must have a proper escort of British soldiers."

"No, thank you. I'll stick to the ones I have. What you can do is get your maintenance people to do a job for me before we return."

"Anything you need."

"Good. I want them to weld a cowcatcher to the front of my lead truck. The rebels kept trying to stop the convoy by dragging trees onto the road or by running in front of us. Either way, this will give them something to think about."

The officer smiled. "Just bring the lorry round and tell them what you want. I'll authorize it."

Johnny looked up at his soldier-ghost. "She's going to push them out of the way with a cowcatcher?"

"That's right. Unfortunately, we can't go back with them because our time has run out. But I can tell you, she brings every one of those prisoners back safely."

"Unbelievable," was all Johnny could think of to say.

"That's why it's important for you to see and understand that heroes are not always men with guns and planes. Women, because their war was different, revealed a different — but no less impressive — kind of courage. Now, it's time for us to leave."

Chapter 15

THE NEXT MORNING, Johnny met Casey in the park. Her outfit of the previous night was gone, but so were her tattered old clothes. Instead, she wore jeans and a thick, chunky sweater, in keeping with the chilly fall day.

She made no reference to her old gear, and Johnny didn't have to. He knew from last night that he had now been accepted as a real friend by this strange girl, who was like no other he had ever known. He could not resist stealing the odd sidelong glance at her as they headed into the park.

They walked in silence for a while, each content with the other's company and the sound of leaves crunching beneath their feet. Casey, her hands thrust deep into her pockets, kicked at a big pile of leaves, sending them scattering.

Suddenly, she raised her head and smiled. "OK, let's hear it. What wonderful adventures did you have last night while I was dreaming about having a fight with my mom?"

Johnny plunged into the story of the nurses from the hospital ship *Lady Nelson*. Casey, who had been listening intently to every word, started to giggle when Johnny got to the part about them having to climb the rope ladders, a giggle that became a howl as he completed the story.

She clapped her hands to her mouth. "No way. You're telling me they had to climb those ladders in skirts with all those sailors standing below? My mother would never do that."

"Neither would mine."

Then Casey became serious. "But then, maybe they would, Johnny. I mean, it seems funny to us now, but this was a war and those women had way more important stuff to get worked up about than that. Why should we think our mothers wouldn't do what they had to, if it was important enough?"

Johnny looked at Casey, impressed at her maturity. "Yeah, I guess you're right. I bet they would, too."

It was at that moment that Johnny, who had been so engrossed in relating his tale that he had been paying little attention to his surroundings, got the odd feeling of eyes boring into his back. Swinging around, he spotted a figure across the park staring at them.

"I don't believe it. That freak-head is in the park," Johnny burst out, remembering the dream he'd been having when his soldier-ghost arrived the previous night.

"What is it? What freak-head?" Casey, who had also swung around, was looking at the figure.

"Jason Lee. He's in my class and he knows everything. At least he thinks he does."

"Is he that bad?"

"It's not that, but he's seen us, so it'll be all over school tomorrow morning."

"So what?"

Johnny was relieved at Casey's nonchalance. But he also detected another meaning in her words, and knew he had to respond.

"Hey, I don't care either, Casey. I'd be crazy not to like having you as my—— "

"Girlfriend?" Casey finished for him, although she knew he'd been about to say "friend."

Johnny's face turned a fierce shade of red. He could feel it from the bottom of his neck all the way up to the tips of his ears. Unable to address what Casey had just said, he replied, "The only thing I'm worried about is that some of them are going to start bugging us."

"Listen, Johnny, I can handle those guys in my sleep. Besides . . ." Casey hesitated, but then plunged on, "I think I kind of like the idea of being your girlfriend." To Johnny's surprise, Casey looked nervous as she waited for his reaction. Miraculously, all of his own nervousness had vanished at her words.

"Me, too, Casey. Me, too," he said, without a trace of a stammer.

"Good. Then let's forget about them and just have fun. How about telling me the rest of what happened last night?" Casey tucked her hand into Johnny's and the pair walked on, with Johnny telling her about Joan Bamford Fletcher.

When he had finished, Casey was quiet for several minutes. Finally she spoke. "You know, Johnny, I'm realizing more and more that we know almost nothing about our grandparents' and great-grandparents' generations and what they did back then. But there's one thing your ghost is showing us: they were strong."

"That's funny. I was just thinking the same thing."

"See? We even think alike."

"Actually, Casey, there's something else I've been thinking about for a while now."

"Oh, do tell. What deep, dark thoughts are tucked away in that mind of yours?"

"No, it's not like that. It's, like, to do with the ghost."

Casey was immediately serious. "What, Johnny?"

"Do you think the ghost is trying to tell me something, like more than just the stories of these Canadian heroes? I mean, the way he keeps reminding me that war is not a nice thing, and last night he said war is not just about men with guns. I keep feeling that there's something more to all this, something more I'm supposed to understand."

Casey stopped and looked at Johnny. After several seconds, she spoke. "The more I know you, the more you surprise me."

"Well, it's just a thought. I've probably got it all wrong, anyway," Johnny finished with an embarrassed laugh.

"No, no. I don't think you have. In fact, I think you're probably right." Casey stood looking at Johnny, deep in thought. Finally, she spoke in a slow, measured voice, as if she were still gathering her thoughts.

"What if he's trying to show you that although war can make ordinary people into heroes, that doesn't mean war is good?"

"Maybe. And that's why he's been showing me so much of the bad stuff that can happen, not just the heroic stuff. To make me realize that even though we should remember what people in the wars did, it would have been a lot better if they never had to do it. I dunno, though. I feel like there's gotta be an even bigger meaning to the soldier-ghost's visits than proving to me how much war sucks — ugh, but I'm too dumb to figure it out."

"Don't you ever tell me again that you are dumb, Johnny Anders. You are one of the smartest guys I've ever met."

"I am?" Johnny was delighted. But then he had another thought. "But one thing I still don't know is, why me?"

"Your soldier-ghost knows that you're smart enough to understand what he's showing you. I bet he knows that somehow you're going to work out what to do with it."

"Yeah?"

"Yeah. Now, I think it's about time we went to your place and did some work on your essay."

Chapter 16

"HELLO, YOU TWO." Johnny's mother smiled at Casey. "Are you staying for lunch?"

"Well, we were going to work in my room," Johnny answered. "I need to get going on my essay."

"Perhaps I'll fix a little something for the two of you and bring it in."

"You don't have to do that, Mrs. Anders," said Casey. "I could just come down and get it when it's ready."

"Nonsense, Casey. You have important work to do. Now get up there and get started."

Listening to this exchange, Johnny felt that Casey could do no wrong as far as his mother was concerned.

Once they were in his room, Casey asked Johnny, "OK, so how far are you with the essay?"

Johnny picked up his notebook and a sheaf of papers. "This is what I have so far." He handed them to Casey, who sat down and started reading through them. She made no comment until she had finished. Then she looked up at Johnny with admiration.

"Johnny, this is really good. Do you know you have a natural flair for writing? You are really starting to capture the drama of the story. Just keep doing what you're doing, and I think your teacher — and the whole class, for that matter — are in for a big surprise."

"You really think it's good?"

"Yes, I do. I really do."

At that moment, Johnny's mother knocked on the door. Casey jumped up to open it, and Mrs. Anders came in with a tray loaded with sandwiches, fruit and drinks.

"How's it going?" she asked, as Casey took the tray and set it on the desk.

Casey opened her mouth to speak, but Johnny beat her to it. "OK, Mom. Casey's just been reading my notes, so we haven't really got started yet."

Casey looked at Johnny, picking up that he didn't want to tell his mother too much.

"Yup, we still have a lot of work to do, Mrs. Anders. Thank you for the lunch. It looks delicious."

"Oh, you're more than welcome. I'd better let you get

back to your work then." With that, Johnny's mother left, closing the door behind her.

"You don't want your parents to know that you're almost finished your essay?"

"If my mom knew that, she'd want to read it. Then she'd start telling me how to make it better."

"I doubt she could have done that. But I understand. Let's eat."

Casey handed Johnny a plate with an egg salad sandwich and took one for herself. They ate in silence, content just to enjoy the food and each other's company.

Once they were finished, Casey took Johnny's plate and placed it back on the tray. "So, update me. Where are you in the book?"

Johnny, conscious of his eggy breath, took a last swallow of his drink before saying, "I just finished the part about where they had to retreat using the train. I can see what you meant about it showing how hard their lives were."

"Totally. What a nightmare!"

"Yeah, I can't believe they had to depend on that old wreck to help them escape. They were so lucky that the Communist train chasing them was just as bad. But it must have been scary with that thing just a couple of miles behind them and firing its cannon at them. And then they had to repair the track, too, as they went along."

"Yeah, it must have been insane. It was lucky that my great-grandfather decided to take along so many refugees.

Without all of them, there's no way they would have been able to delay the Communists. Like while the women refugees were off the train collecting wood for fuel, the men went back along the tracks and ripped up the railway lines. That was really cool."

"Yeah, you're right. And if it wasn't for all those people there to help out, the whole train could have been lost the night your great-grandfather's coach caught fire and he lost all his stuff."

"True, but I think the worst part of the journey was when some of the refugees' babies got typhoid, and he had to order their parents to throw the dead ones off the train because it was too dangerous to stop and bury them."

"Yeah, that was the worst part of all."

"Still, I think they were really lucky they made it to that place on the coast, Sevastopol."

"Definitely. I think the aircraft mechanic they had driving that engine had a lot to do with their escape. It's crazy how when the Communist train started to get too close, he managed to get the extra speed out of the thing without blowing it up."

"True, Johnny. I'd forgotten about him. You know, that one little story says so much about the difficulties they had to face, and how they dealt with them. Don't you think?"

"Yeah, I guess so. Do you remember after they got to their new airfield at that place, what was it called, Dankjoi? Anyway, your great-grandfather led a mission to bomb a couple of Communist trains pretty soon after they arrived, and his plane got hit by ground fire, and he was forced to make an emergency landing."

"Right," Casey interrupted excitedly. "And because he knew he didn't have enough power to get off the ground, because of the damage, he drove it across the fields to get back to their airfield at Dankjoi. That was so cool."

"I thought it was amazing that even though they must have known by that time they were on the losing side, they still kept on fighting."

"Even when they thought they were going home, after they arrived at Sevastopol and saw the British warship."

"OK. I've got to put that stuff in the essay if anyone's going to understand what it was really like."

The two spent the rest of the afternoon going through Johnny's work, with Johnny doing the writing and Casey only offering advice when necessary. They barely noticed the time ticking by until Johnny's mother called up to remind them it was close to suppertime.

Chapter 17

ALTHOUGH JOHNNY never knew where his soldier-ghost was going to take him on his strange trips into the past, he never would have guessed he would end up in the middle of the ocean.

"We're on board His Majesty's Canadian Ship *Valleyfield*."

"Where is she going?"

"Home, actually. She's coming back from convoy duty and is taking her group of corvette convoy escorts back to St. John's for a well earned break."

"So she's the senior ship then?"

"That's right. The *Valleyfield* is a frigate and slightly larger than a corvette, so she has the officer commanding the squadron on board."

Well aware by this time that everywhere his soldier-ghost had taken him was to see some kind of heroic deed in battle, Johnny asked, "If she is just going back to harbour, why are we here?"

"I wondered when you were going to ask that. Being near home doesn't automatically guarantee a ship's safety, as we shall soon see. We are also going to witness a different kind of bravery. You see, with seamen, because they are all confined on ship, bravery tends to be more a shared thing. When things go wrong, they are all in it together."

As Johnny looked across the bridge of the ship at the sailors, who were muffled up in sheepskin-lined watch coats or duffle coats, he marvelled at how he remained completely outside the cold. At the same time, he wondered what was going to happen to these men.

He didn't have long to wait. Suddenly there was a flurry of activity on the bridge. One of the officers had switched on a loudspeaker and a humming sound could be heard coming from it.

"That is the ASDIC machine, an anti-submarine detector that has picked up something."

"A submarine?"

"Worse, I'm afraid."

BAM! A huge explosion erupted from the side of the ship, sending flames shooting into the sky.

"What happened?" Johnny gasped as the men on the bridge and decks were all sent flying.

"She's just been torpedoed."

"She's in big trouble then?"

Johnny didn't need an answer, for at that moment the ship began to break apart and oil started pouring into the sea. Within seconds, the stern of the ship broke completely away and began sinking.

The captain rushed up on deck, took one look around and immediately gave the order to abandon ship. His order came not a moment too soon, for, to Johnny's horror, the front end of the ship started to disappear, her bow having first risen up from the water as the ship stood on end.

The men still on the bridge were left with no choice but to jump into the icy water. Then Johnny spotted three men climbing up the remaining part of the stern that hadn't disappeared below the waves.

"Now you are going to see the collective bravery of the sailor," said the soldier-ghost. "Those three men are trying to disarm the depth charges at the stern. They are anti-submarine weapons that are always kept armed, and will explode as soon as the water covers them."

"Why don't they just leave them and save themselves?"

"Because those three men, Leading Seaman Brown, Able Seaman Woods and Ordinary Seaman Brown, know that if those charges explode, what's left of the crew in the water will be either killed by the explosion or burned to death when the oil catches fire."

Johnny watched, mesmerized, as the three men worked

frantically on the depth charges until the stern finally surrendered to the sea, sucking all three men down with it. They
must have succeeded in disarming the depth charges as there
was no explosion.

In the water, the remains of the *Valleyfield*'s crew, who
hadn't had time to get to a life raft before abandoning ship,
were thrashing around trying to reach one of the few rafts
that had been launched, their bodies covered with the
thick, black oil that was rapidly covering the water.

"What will happen to them?"

For once, his soldier-ghost didn't answer him directly,
but touched his hand as he spoke. "Come, there's another
part of this tragedy still to be played out."

Johnny found himself standing on the bridge of another
ship. On this bridge were a group of officers, some with
binoculars trained at a spot out in the ocean. One officer
was speaking excitedly to the captain.

"We were checking our station position with the *Valleyfield*, sir, when the explosion occurred and we saw a great
column of smoke and steam coming from where she was."

Johnny's soldier-ghost spoke. "We are now going to see
how, in the heat of a crisis, the best of us can make a mistake. Unfortunately, this one will prove very costly. This ship
is the HMCS *Giffard*, one of the corvettes in the *Valleyfield*'s
group, and the officers have just witnessed the explosion on
their command ship. Their captain is a man named Petersen, a capable officer but one who has never faced a situa-
tion like this."

"What's he going to do?"

"We are about to see."

Captain Petersen stood for several minutes, unsure of his next move. Finally he made up his mind and ordered his ship to close in on the *Valleyfield*, at the same time calling his command ship on the radio transmitter to see if he could establish contact. But he was already too late. There was only dead silence.

"Have you noticed the captain's error yet?" Johnny's soldier-ghost looked down at him enquiringly.

Johnny shook his head.

"He hasn't contacted the other ships in the group to let them know what has happened, and they are still sailing on to St. John's, oblivious of the disaster that has befallen their command ship."

"Is that bad?"

"Very, as we'll soon see."

Soon, the *Giffard* reached the scene and eventually located the survivors in the oil-covered water.

"Now, Captain Petersen faces a dilemma of his own making, because somewhere nearby is the U-boat that torpedoed the *Valleyfield*. If he stops his own ship to pick up survivors, he will be a sitting duck for the U-boat. To add to his dilemma, he is about to compound his earlier mistake by yet again not notifying the rest of the group what happened. So he doesn't have the help he desperately needs from the other ships in the group who could take care of the U-boat, which would allow him to stop safely and collect the survivors."

"What will he do?"

"We are about to find out."

Johnny watched, mesmerized again by the drama playing out before his eyes. Once again, Captain Petersen seemed to be unsure what to do, as precious minutes ticked away.

Finally he spoke. "Slow ahead, Engine Room. Stand by to pick up survivors." The *Giffard* slowed to a crawl. It was still a risky move, and even at that speed the plan proved hopeless. The men in the water were already paralyzed with cold as they tried to grab the nets and ropes the crew of the *Giffard* had dropped over the side. The movement of the ship proved too much for the frozen men, and they couldn't hold on for more than a second or two.

As Captain Petersen watched the men falling away from the ship as fast as they grabbed the nets, the hopelessness of his plan seemed to jolt his memory. He issued an order to his radio operator: "Signal the rest of the squadron, *Valleyfield* torpedoed."

"Will the other ships come to help?" Johnny asked.

"Oh yes, eventually, but if you heard his message, you will be aware he still hasn't told them where the *Giffard* and *Valleyfield* are. Not that it could help him now even if they had clear directions, because they are already too far away to arrive in time to solve the captain's dilemma."

Johnny was far too engrossed in what was happening to grasp the significance of Captain Petersen's all-too-brief message, but he nodded anyway.

"Now the captain must make one of two decisions.

Either he stops the *Giffard* completely to pick up the survivors, which would put his own ship and crew in terrible danger, or he must go after the U-boat and at the very least assure himself that it has left the area before he can risk stopping."

Johnny could see the agony on Captain Petersen's face as he gave the order. "Resume speed, Number One, and take her back to previous course."

The *Giffard* picked up speed and pulled away from the horrified survivors, still struggling in the icy waters.

Johnny must have shown his own shock and dismay at the captain's decision, because his soldier-ghost placed a hand on his shoulder. "He really had no choice, you know. What we have just witnessed is one of the great tragedies of war. Young men, many new to their jobs, are forced to make life-and-death decisions, sometimes in a matter of seconds and without sufficient information. All they can do is their best, but sometimes mistakes are made that result in a larger tragedy.

"Historians, of course, with the advantage of hindsight, can always point out what should have happened. But that doesn't mean that, given the same conditions, they would have done any better."

"Will he come back and save the survivors?"

"Oh yes. The other ships will finally arrive and take over the search for the U-boat, which will enable the *Giffard* to return and complete the rescue."

"Do they all get saved?"

"Sadly, not all. The icy water will claim many. But let's jump ahead. I want you to see that even in the midst of tragedy, small miracles sometimes occur."

With a touch of his soldier-ghost's hand, Johnny and the *Giffard* were back among the survivors of the *Valleyfield*. But this time, knowing he was protected, Captain Petersen virtually stopped the ship, just leaving enough forward movement to keep it drifting gently among the survivors. His crew began hauling the men to safety, while he launched his sea-boat to collect the survivors farther out.

The *Giffard* came alongside one of the floats from the *Valleyfield*. It was full of men in duffle coats all huddled together, except for one man lying in the bottom, who was clad in nothing but a pair of shorts and a life jacket.

Once they had pulled the raft on board, the rescuers realized that everyone in it was dead. They laid the bodies on deck, and immediately returned to the more urgent matter of saving the living.

A few minutes later one of the crewman walked past the piled bodies and spotted movement among them.

"Hey, over here. There's one still alive," he yelled. Several more men rushed over and gently removed a man from the pile of corpses. To Johnny's astonishment, it was the seaman who was wearing nothing but his underwear.

"See what I mean? Even in the midst of the worst tragedies, miracles can occur."

"Is he going to be all right?"

"Yes, he will recover."

"Do the others sink the U-boat?"

"Unfortunately, miracles tend to happen rarely. The U-boat has already taken off for safer waters and will live to sink more ships."

Johnny's face must have reflected his anger at the news, for his soldier-ghost spoke again. "I know how you feel, but it's a sad fact of war that the good guys don't win every time. Come, it's time for you to return."

Chapter 18

JUST AS JOHNNY HAD feared, there was a group of his class-mates standing around waiting for Casey and him when they arrived at school Monday morning. Jason Lee was front and centre.

"See, what did I tell you?" Jason yelled, pointing at Casey, who was wearing another pair of jeans and a green sweater.

"Where did he find her?" Eddie Roy wondered out loud. "I never seen her around here before."

One of the girls, who had been peering closely at Casey, suddenly laughed. "Oh yes, you have. That's Casey Colli-shaw. She and Johnny have been hanging out for a while now. Hi, Casey." The girl waved.

"Are you telling me that's the same girl who dresses like a bag lady?" Eddie asked in disbelief.

Casey turned and smiled sweetly at Eddie. "Actually, yes." Then, thoroughly enjoying the stir she had created, she deliberately took Johnny's hand, and the pair of them strolled past the gaping boys and girls.

Johnny, beaming, whispered, "Boy, that was so cool. I've never enjoyed coming to school as much as that. Did you see their faces?"

"So, did I do you proud, Johnny Anders?"

"Are you kidding?" Johnny burst out. "I'll never forget today, not ever."

All morning during classes, Johnny's classmates kept throwing glances at him. But no one said a word to him about Casey, as if they were still struggling to believe what they had seen that morning.

Rather than feeling embarrassed, as he would have just a short time ago, Johnny found himself thoroughly enjoying the experience. He couldn't wait to tell Casey about it during lunch break.

He found her surrounded by a group of girls, all chattering excitedly to her. One girl, Jenny Klein, who was dominating the conversation, spotted Johnny and grinned, immediately raising her voice so that he could hear her. "Yeah, well if you say so, but I wouldn't be caught dead with that geek. And, anyway I'm sure he's girl-challenged."

Johnny couldn't see Casey's face, but he could hear her

voice. "Well, that's just fine then, isn't it? I'll keep my girl-challenged geek and you can keep your muscle-bound jock." Jenny, whose boyfriend was Eddie Roy, sucked in her breath.

With that, Casey broke away from the group and, with a wave of her hand, ran across to Johnny, leaving Jenny with her mouth hanging open.

"How did your morning go?" Casey asked.

"Best I ever had."

"Did you get teased about your new girlfriend?"

"That was the funny part. Nobody said a word. They just kept looking at me, kind of confused."

"Same with me, except for that Jenny Klein." Casey glanced at the girl she had just exchanged words with. Jenny was still glaring at her.

Johnny and Casey grinned at each other, both revelling in the stir they had caused.

Johnny's afternoon followed the same pattern as the morning, with the rest of the class throwing him puzzled glances but no one saying a word. He strolled out of school that afternoon with a distinct swagger in his walk, and found Casey surrounded by the same group of girls as at lunch break. Just as before, she broke away at the sight of him and came over.

"I'm never going to forget this day," Johnny said.

"That's the second time you said that, so I guess the afternoon was as good as the morning."

Johnny smiled, a little sheepishly. "Yes, but it is all thanks to you."

"Then I'm never going to forget this day, either. Now let's get home. I'm dying to hear about where your soldier-ghost took you this time."

———∿∿∿———

"So, what happened last night?" Casey asked, the moment Johnny sat down. She was already curled up on her bed, her feet tucked underneath her.

"It was another big surprise."

"Surprise, how?"

"We were on a ship, a frigate that got torpedoed."

"Oh my God. What happened?"

As Johnny recounted the events that he had witnessed the previous night, Casey sat even more still than usual, absorbing every word without comment until Johnny had finished.

"You know, Johnny, I've read so much about the things that happened, both in that war and the others my great-grandfather fought in, but I've never really been able to feel what it must have been like, until now."

"Me neither. Well, I didn't have any idea at all, 'cause I didn't ever try. I wish . . ." Johnny hesitated, "No, it's stupid. I couldn't do it."

Casey sat up, her green eyes sparkling. "Do what? What do you mean?"

"It's just that I thought . . . maybe when I grow up, that I could write about all this, you know, properly. But I couldn't."

Casey's eyes flashed. "If you don't stop putting yourself

down, I'm going to slap you. Don't you get it? That essay you're doing is awesome — you're a natural born writer."

Casey suddenly stopped and slapped her leg. "Of course. Don't you see? This is what else you're supposed to discover: that you can write about it."

"You really think so?" Johnny's face showed doubt.

"How long have you known me, Johnny?"

"Not long, but it seems like forever."

"And in all this time, you're telling me that you haven't figured out that I never say anything just to make someone happy?"

"I should have by now, shouldn't I," Johnny said, with mock solemnity.

Casey burst into laughter.

"It's not that I don't believe you," he continued. "It's just that no one has ever believed that I could do anything special — not even my parents — and I guess I just got used to it and never bothered trying. So it's kinda hard to start thinking differently now."

"You've got to learn to believe in yourself, Johnny, because there's always someone out there ready to put you down. Not your parents, of course, but other people, especially at school. They do it because it makes them feel better about themselves. Now let's forget all that and get back to the essay. Where are you with it?"

"About at the end, I think. But I found one more piece to use. I thought that part about that ataman guy who tried to order them to leave the country really should be in there, because it was another example of the problems they had to face, on top of the actual fighting."

"Oh yeah, I remember. An ataman was like a local government official who controlled certain areas."

"This one seemed to think he was in charge of the war, and wanted to do things his way. I bet he was surprised when your great-grandfather arrived with his armed escort and arrested him."

"Yeah, that must have dented his ego. Luckily, there were people around more powerful than the ataman. They let my great-grandfather arrest him before he could do more damage."

"That's why I wanted to use that story. Like I said before, if I'm going to do this right, I have to show all the problems they had to deal with, on top of trying to fight a war."

Casey beamed. "See? You're thinking just like a writer."

"But don't you think, Casey, that really, none of those flyers should ever have been sent to Russia in the first place?"

"I think you just came up with the ending for your essay, Johnny. Isn't that the real point in all this?"

"I never thought of it like that, but, yeah, I guess you're right."

At that moment Casey's mother called up the stairs. "It's getting late, you two. I think your mother will be phoning soon to find out where you are, Johnny."

Johnny looked at his watch. "Oh jeez, five-thirty. I didn't think it was that late."

"This is getting to be a habit, Johnny Anders. You'll make my mom suspicious if you keep this up." Casey gave him a roguish look. Then she uncurled herself from the bed and headed for the door, calling out, "Coming, Mom."

Chapter 19

ALTHOUGH JOHNNY couldn't be sure just by looking at them, he guessed one of the two Chinese coolies shuffling along the dusty track was Bill Chong. He noticed one of them was using a walking stick made of bamboo.

As if he had read his mind, the soldier-ghost spoke. "The one with the walking stick is Bill and the other man is a guide he has employed for this trip. Bill is travelling a route he has never used before and it is full of Japanese patrols."

"Why has he come this way?"

"Because he is carrying very important intelligence from the British consul in Macau, and needs to get it to Kukong as soon as possible. This is a much more direct route back into Free China than he would normally use for his missions, but it's also much riskier, as you are about to witness."

As the soldier-ghost finished speaking, Johnny heard the sound of men approaching. Bill and his guide immediately dived into the bushes. A Japanese patrol, consisting of ten soldiers, one officer plus a dozen coolies, appeared around the corner. Each of the coolies was carrying an ammunition box on his shoulders.

As Bill and his guide watched from the bushes, one of the coolies stumbled and dropped his box. The box rolled over and flew open, but all that fell out was a load of rocks.

Bill craned forward to get a better look at this astonishing evidence of the dire state of the Japanese army — a move that proved to be his undoing.

The officer heard the movement and whirled around to where the two men were hiding, barking orders to his men. Four unslung their rifles and ran toward the bushes, dragging Bill and the guide out before they had a chance to run. Both men were hauled over to where the officer was standing and flung at his feet, Bill's walking stick falling to the ground and rolling back across the path in the process.

The officer drew his sword and shouted something. The guide, being the only one of the two who could speak some Japanese, said something back. Not satisfied with his answer, the officer hit the guide across the head with the flat of his sword, and shouted at him once more. The guide said something in reply, but again, the answer did not satisfy the officer. He hit him again, this time cutting his head open.

Then he turned to two of his men and pointed at Bill. The men dragged him over to a tree stump and tied his hands behind him. They then pushed him down so his neck was resting on the stump. The officer raised his sword over his head. Johnny gasped and clapped his hands over his mouth.

Just as the officer was poised to bring the sword down, the guide shouted something.

The officer whirled around and lowered his sword. Bill's guide shouted again, and the officer walked over, reached into the man's tattered tunic and pulled out a scrap of paper. After reading it, the officer, to Johnny's astonishment, said something to his men, who cut Bill Chong and the guide loose. Then the officer gestured at them to go.

The guide immediately headed for the jungle while Bill ran across the dusty path, fishing around in the foliage until he found his cane. Snatching it up, he followed the guide into the jungle.

"What happened? And why did Bill bother stopping to find his cane?"

Johnny's soldier-ghost chuckled. "Because inside that cane are the documents he's taking back to his boss at the British Army Aid Group's headquarters in Kukong. As for what happened, you will see. Come."

With a touch of his soldier-ghost's hand they caught up with Bill and the guide. Expecting to see the two men laughing and clapping each other on the back at their miraculous escape, Johnny was taken aback by the fact that Bill was walking several paces behind the guide and eyeing him warily.

"Bill has no idea yet what happened back there and is now highly suspicious of his guide. He is wondering if he is a Japanese agent sent to infiltrate the organization, and if he, Bill, is taking him right to where he wants to go."

"What's he going to do?"

"We are about to find out by taking a leap forward to Kukong." With that now-familiar touch, Johnny found himself in the street of a large, bustling town. As he looked around, he saw Bill Chong and his guide shuffling down the street toward them. They headed into a building just a few yards away, and with the soldier-ghost's touch, he and the soldier-ghost followed.

Johnny found himself standing in a hallway. A few feet away Bill Chong was talking animatedly to a man in army fatigues while the guide shouted wildly at Bill, waving his arms. The sentry grabbed the guide's arm and propelled him into the room he had been guarding. Bill, Johnny and the soldier-ghost followed.

Seated at a battered desk, a distinguished looking man with a distinct air of authority looked up from his writing. His name was Edwin Ride, and he was head of the British Army Aid Group. Seeing Bill standing there, he looked enquiringly at his most successful agent, knowing he would not normally bring a guide into the room to report on a mission. "What is it, Bill?"

Bill Chong then recited the events of his miraculous escape. The man spoke to the guide, who fished out the grubby slip of paper and handed it over, at the same time chattering excitedly.

Only then did Johnny realize that it wasn't a note at all, but a very soiled business card.

As the guide finished speaking, Edwin Ride started to laugh. The laugh quickly grew into a roar. "Did you get that, Bill? My God, but you should keep this man around. He just saved both your lives by conning the Japanese officer into believing you were both Japanese agents working for this major based in Hong Kong. He did it with this card." Edwin Ride waved the card at Bill. "Your very smart guide found it and thought it might come in handy one day. He didn't know just how handy it would be."

Johnny looked at his soldier-ghost, surprised that a Japanese officer could be fooled so easily.

"Ah, I see you are confused by this. Well, just remember that the Japanese were trained to accept all orders from a superior officer without question. To challenge an order would almost guarantee one's execution. Well, the same training applies to officers and, clearly, the man who captured them wasn't about to risk bucking a major in intelligence. Easier to let them go and say nothing."

"So, the card belongs to an intelligence officer?"

The soldier-ghost shook his head. "Oh, no. The card actually belongs to a retired Japanese army major. Intelligence officers don't go around broadcasting what they do. But the officer who captured Bill and his guide wouldn't have known for sure whether the guide was telling the truth or not, so he erred on the side of caution and self-preservation. Come, we still have another stop tonight."

A quick touch of the hand and Johnny found himself standing inside a building with huge furnaces roaring away as men, sweaty and blackened, staggered back and forth carrying steel girders.

"Shintetsu steel mill in Nagata, Japan, where our friend Geoff Marston and many of his colleagues have wound up. That's him stoking the furnace over there."

Johnny's soldier-ghost pointed across the huge shop. Geoff Marston looked nothing like the well-kept man they had last visited in Bowen Road Hospital. Now he looked just like the emaciated prisoner Johnny had first seen in North Point Camp.

"They were brought here from Hong Kong to work as slave labour in the mill," the soldier-ghost explained.

"How do they manage to work like this? They look like they're starving."

"Fear." Johnny's soldier-ghost spit out the word with bitterness, as he pointed to a short, stocky Japanese walking around the mill, a large stick swinging ominously in his hand.

"It is their only hope of surviving, because once they become incapable of working, they also become disposable."

Johnny shuddered.

Then the soldier-ghost smiled. "But come, I want to show you the incredible spirit of these prisoners and one of the seemingly crazy things they do just to help themselves survive." A touch on Johnny's hand and they were standing inside a long, gloomy building lined with tiers of wooden-slatted bunks and very little else. Sprawled on the bunks were some of the men they had seen in the mill.

"Hey, hurry up with the grub, Joe. It's my turn," a man yelled from one of the bunks.

Johnny looked up at his soldier-ghost, for there wasn't any food to be seen.

"Watch," the soldier-ghost said.

"OK, OK, Fred, I was just enjoying a great big sirloin steak with fries."

With that, Joe got up and flung a grubby magazine across to Fred.

Consumed with curiosity, Johnny looked again at his soldier-ghost for an explanation.

"It's an old food magazine someone found. Every night they take turns picking out a meal and imagining themselves back home eating it. That magazine is as important to their survival as a water bottle is to a person lost in the desert, because it gives them hope, something to hang on to."

"And do they . . . survive?"

"Not all. But as impossible as it might seem now, most of them will, as we are about to see, because our friend Geoff Marston is going to give us one last demonstration of their amazing resilience."

One touch of his soldier-ghost's hand and they were back outside in the compound. But immediately Johnny noticed that something was different.

All the men were wandering around, looking dazed. There wasn't a guard in sight. Then Johnny saw something that brought back memories of the night his soldier-ghost had taken him to the prison camp in Bankinang to see Joan Bamford Fletcher evacuate the prisoners. The gate to the compound was wide open.

"What the hell is going on?" one of the men asked no one in particular.

"Beats me," said Geoff Marston.

Suddenly the drone of a plane could be heard. The men looked up as a huge four-engine bomber appeared in the sky with a banner streaming from its tail.

"My God, it's American. What does that banner say?"

They soon got their answer as the plane straightened and came low over the compound: "War Over. Happy Days Are Here Again. Soldiers Coming To Take You Home."

The prisoners barely had time to absorb the implications of the message before the plane doors flew open and containers began falling to the ground. A rush ensued and the prisoners ripped the containers open, spilling out more food than they had seen in four long years. With the food came carton after carton of cigarettes.

Pretty soon, the men were gorging themselves and smoking, both at the same time. Because they hadn't eaten so much food for years, some of them became ill and threw up.

After collecting his share of food and cigarettes, Geoff Marston wandered over to the open gate with another prisoner.

"Never thought I'd see this day. Did you, Reg?"

"No, Geoff. Never did."

Geoff kept looking at the open gate and rubbing his face, which was covered with a ragged beard.

"The hell with it. I'm going to get a haircut and shave."

"Are you mad, Geoff? You know what those people in the town are like. They nearly lynched us when we were brought here."

"I bet they wouldn't dare touch us now."

"Well, if you want to get killed after all we've survived, good luck. I'm staying here till the soldiers come."

Geoff grinned at him, then walked through the gate and into the town.

His reception was more surprising than he had expected. The people in the town all stepped back as he approached and bowed.

He found a barbershop and received the same reception, the owner bowing obsequiously and ushering him to a chair.

Johnny looked on in astonishment as the man he had followed through four years of hardship, brutality and near-death was given a haircut and shave.

"I think that demonstrates nicely what I meant about resilience. Now, we are at the end of our journey and my time has run out. All I can hope now is that you take the little I have been able to show you and search for the rest yourself, then put it all to some use."

Johnny stood very still at his soldier-ghost's words. He had become so used to these journeys back into history that he had barely thought about them ending. Trying to extend the moment, he blurted, "But what about Bill Chong?"

"Oh, Bill survives the war, too, and is awarded the British Empire Medal for bravery. He stays in Hong Kong for some time, where he and another man open a second-hand camera shop. After about six months, he gets a visit from two agents from MI5, Britain's top overseas intelligence service. They re-recruit Bill, and send him back into the same jungles to spy on what the British thought was a new enemy, one that will emerge in the form of Communist China. Come, it really is time for you to return to your world."

"Can I ask one more question before we go?"

"One."

"What about you?"

Johnny's soldier-ghost chuckled. "I thought you might have guessed. I'm the Unknown Soldier, the one who lies at every war memorial in the world and represents all those who died and were never found. Now it really is time."

Chapter 20

JOHNNY'S FIRST SENSATION on waking was one of loss, but he couldn't think why. Then he rolled over and saw the bedroom wall through which he had passed to go on so many adventures.

Slowly he got out of bed, went over to the wall and thumped it, just as he had on that first day. But there was a difference this time. This time he knew that it would forever remain solid, even when the night came, and every other night from then on.

He picked up his clothes and wandered out of his room, the uppermost thought in his mind that he must not let it all fade away.

"Johnny, you're doing it again."

"Doing what, Mom?"

"Pushing your breakfast around. Will you please eat up? I have to get to work."

"Sorry, Mom."

"You're quiet this morning. Anything wrong?"

"What? No, nothing, Mom. I was just thinking about the essay, that's all."

"Well, you've been pushing that breakfast around for the last five minutes. You're not coming down with something, are you?"

"No, Mom, I'm fine. Honest."

Johnny concentrated on getting his breakfast down before his mother could probe him further. As soon as he had finished, he grabbed his school things, put on his coat and left. He felt an overwhelming need to see Casey and tell her that the soldier-ghost would no longer be appearing.

He caught her on her way to school and spilled out his news. But apart from a perfunctory "Oh," Casey seemed to have nothing to say. They walked in silence for some time, both with their hands deep in their pockets, hunched into their winter coats against a day that seemed to be reacting to their mood, with lowering clouds and a bitingly cold wind.

Finally, Casey found her voice. "I guess we both thought that it wouldn't end. But it was kind of dumb, wasn't it? Because we knew it had to."

"Yeah, 'course we did, but I just wasn't thinking about it. And I was really surprised, though he said he only had time to show me certain parts, and that it was up to me to find out about the rest and do something with it."

Casey smiled. "Of course. You're right, Johnny. That's the most important thing — that you don't waste what you've learned."

"No way I'm going to do that. I have to use it. I will use it."

Casey squeezed his arm. "Hey, do you realize that is the first time you made up your mind on your own?"

Johnny beamed. "Yeah, it is, isn't it? But I wouldn't have done it if I hadn't met you."

"Yes, you would. But you know, there's something we've both forgotten."

"What?"

"That if it wasn't for all this we might never have become friends."

"Jeez, how could I forget the best thing that ever happened to me?"

"And to me, Johnny."

"Really?"

"Really. So let's stop moping about it ending and remember all the good things that have happened since your ghost appeared."

By the time the two friends reached school, they were feeling much better. Their spirits were lifted even higher when some of their classmates actually greeted them with waves and "hi's," though Jason Lee still looked at Johnny and Casey as if he couldn't believe his eyes.

—◈—

"OK, tell me where you went last night," Casey burst out as soon as they were in her room and she had arranged herself in her usual position on the bed. "And don't leave out anything, especially seeing as how it was the last time."

Johnny carefully recited everything that happened, not missing a single detail.

As always, Casey listened intently to every word without interrupting. That is, until Johnny got to the part about Geoff Marston and his trip to the barber.

She clapped her hands to her mouth and started to giggle. "He actually walked into town and asked a Japanese barber to give him a haircut and shave? Oh, that is so cool."

"Yeah, that's what I thought."

"And Johnny." Casey was serious again. "Doesn't it also say a lot about these men? I mean, that one of them could think about something like a haircut after all he had suffered?"

"That's exactly what the ghost said. You know, Casey, I really hated it when my dad came up with this idea of going to the Remembrance Day ceremony on my birthday. But it's all different now."

"Remembrance Day is your birthday? You never told me that. That means your birthday is in two days!"

"I guess I just forgot, with all the other stuff that's been going on. Anyway, my dad said it was important that I go, because I was born on such a historic day."

Casey looked thoughtful. "Do you believe in destiny, Johnny?"

"Never really thought about it."

"Well, you should, because all of this seems like it was supposed to happen."

"What, like us meeting and all that?"

"All of it. Don't you think? Anyway, where are we going to meet Thursday? We always go pretty early and stand right opposite the memorial, because what I like the most is watching the old soldiers when they have the two minutes' silence. There's something about the way they look, like they're sort of not there."

"OK. I'll tell my dad we should meet you there."

"Great. I'll see you on Thursday."

Johnny looked a bit surprised. "What about tomorrow?"

"Can't tomorrow, Johnny. I've got something I have to do."

"Oh." Johnny looked a bit deflated.

"Hey, don't go sulky on me. It's the only day I won't have seen you, except when I had to go shopping with my mom," Casey said in a teasing tone.

Johnny immediately smiled. "Sorry, I just like being with you, that's all."

"Me, too. But this is important, and I need some space. Now get yourself home. I'll see you Thursday."

"OK." Johnny beamed, Casey's first two words not lost on him, as he bounced to his feet.

They went downstairs together and Casey opened the front door. With one last wave, Johnny walked down the driveway toward home.

Chapter 21

JOHNNY WOKE THE following morning with a bad case of the blues. For the first time in days, he had neither his nocturnal adventures, nor a meeting with Casey, to look forward to. He decided to read more of Casey's great-grandfather's book.

Until now, Johnny had focused his reading almost exclusively on the part dealing with the Russian Revolution. Now he turned to the beginning and Collishaw's first taste of war. Immediately he was swept back into the past he had so recently vacated, as Casey's great-grandfather took him through the air battles that had raged over the Western Front in 1917 and 1918, then through his third war, in

Persia, where he had been sent to help the Shah protect the country from invaders, and eventually into the arid deserts of North Africa in the Second World War.

This final conflict was to be Collishaw's last and most prestigious, for he was put in charge of all Fighter Command's squadrons for the Desert Campaign, as it became known. It would earn him the rank of Air Vice Marshal by the time he retired in 1943.

It was late afternoon by the time Johnny read the final chapter of this remarkable story, and his blue mood had completely disappeared.

Chapter 22

NOVEMBER ELEVENTH dawned cold and grey, but Johnny barely noticed. To the complete surprise of his parents, he appeared in the kitchen before his mother was halfway through cooking breakfast.

"Good Lord, what brought this on?" his father said, lowering his paper.

His mother turned from her cooking and smiled at her son. "Happy birthday, dear," the smile turning to a frown as her eyes fastened on her husband.

"Yes, happy birthday, son." Johnny's father disappeared back behind his paper.

"Thanks Mom, thanks Dad," Johnny replied, hiding a grin at the silent rebuke his father had just received.

Once breakfast was on the table, they all sat down to eat.

"By the way, Johnny, I hope you didn't forget to invite Casey back for your birthday supper?" A piece of toast stopped halfway to Johnny's mouth.

"Er . . . yeah, 'course I didn't forget."

"You don't seem that certain."

"Yes, I am, Mom."

"I should hope so."

Just at that moment the doorbell rang.

"I'll get it." Johnny jumped up from the table, eager to escape his mother's questions, which he knew all too well could be relentless.

Flinging open the door, he froze at the sight of the subject of his mother's questions standing there.

"Are you going to make a habit of leaving me on the doorstep?" Casey asked.

"No, of course not. I just wasn't expecting to see you until later."

"Well, I didn't think that would be the best place to wish you a happy birthday. It would be a little too public." With that, Casey bent forward and kissed Johnny, leaving him in an even bigger state of shock. He came out of it only when his mother called from the kitchen, "Who is it, Johnny?"

"It's Casey, Mom."

His mother appeared. "Casey. This is a nice surprise. We thought you were going straight to the parade."

"I was, but I wanted to bring Johnny his present beforehand, so I asked my dad to drop me off here and I would get a ride with you guys. Is that OK?"

"Oh, I don't think that will be a problem. Come on in."

Casey stepped into the hall and placed a large, brightly coloured bag on the floor. She opened it and pulled out a package wrapped in shiny paper. Handing it to Johnny, she said, "I hope you like it. You didn't give me much time."

Mrs. Anders swung around to face her son. "Did you leave it until the last minute to invite Casey to your birthday supper? Really Johnny, you are the limit."

"No, it's fine, Mrs. Anders, honest. I guess we kept working so hard on the project, we hardly talked about anything else until the last couple of days." Casey crossed her fingers as the white lie rolled off her tongue. "Well, open it then," she said, turning back to Johnny.

As Johnny started to remove the wrapping, Casey, nibbling at her lower lip, looked on with an apprehensive expression. Johnny pulled away the rest of the paper and stared at the present.

"You don't like it?"

"Are you kidding? It's awesome. I've envied your pictures ever since I first saw them, and now you're giving me this one!" Johnny swung the picture around to his mother. "This is a picture of Casey's great-grandfather, you know, the one who was a famous fighter ace in the First World War and who also fought in the Russian Revolution. He served in the Second World War too and became an Air Vice Marshal."

"That's why I couldn't see you yesterday, Johnny," Casey said. "I had to think of something to get you for your birthday. When I decided on the photograph, I had to find a print shop that could make a really good copy. Then I had to find a frame for it."

Johnny's mother wiped her hands and took the framed print. "You must be quite proud of having such a famous ancestor," she said to Casey.

"May I see?" His father had come into the hall, and reached for the photograph. After he looked at it, he said to Casey. "You know, I had no idea Canadians actually fought in the Russian Revolution until Johnny told me." Then, turning to his son, he said, "Well, thanks to this girl, you certainly seem to have learned a lot of history — much more than I ever knew."

"If only you knew how much," Johnny whispered to himself.

"You guys better get going if you want to get a good spot for the parade."

"Oh, no need to worry, Mrs. Anders. My dad will save us a space, and I know where he'll be. Aren't you coming?"

"I'd love to, Casey, but I still need to make Johnny's birthday cake. But you can tell me all about it later."

—✧—

Casey led them to the spot where her father was waiting.

"Ah, good, you're here. It's getting more and more difficult to keep a bit of space," he said.

Johnny's father reached out a hand to Casey's father. "So, you are the father of this wonder girl who seems to have somehow turned my son into a keen student."

"Well, I don't know about that. But Casey has always had strong opinions and she is not afraid to express them. She also, as you must have noticed by her dress habits, likes to defy convention."

Casey flushed. "Dad, stop it."

Johnny's father was puzzled. "I'm sorry, I don't follow. Casey, as far as I have seen, dresses very well."

"Would everyone please stop discussing me as if I were somewhere else, instead of standing right here?" Casey's green eyes were flashing.

"Quite right," Johnny's father said. "Very rude of us."

Casey's father, realizing, with some relief, that his daughter had never appeared at the Anders' home in her usual tattered garb, quickly changed the subject.

"Your wife not coming?"

"She couldn't make it. She's busy making Johnny's birthday cake."

"Oh, so Johnny was born on Remembrance Day. That's pretty interesting."

The conversation between the two men then turned to other subjects, allowing Casey and Johnny the chance to talk.

"You forgot, didn't you? You forgot to invite your girlfriend to your own birthday. I'm furious," Casey whispered, the twinkle in her eye belying the rebuke in her voice.

"No, I didn't. I wouldn't. It was just that, like, with everything that's happened, I'd even forgotten about my birthday until it came up on Tuesday. Honest."

"OK, you're off the hook this time. But you'd better not forget mine."

"Well, I don't know yours anyway."

"Don't worry. I'll remind you every day when it gets close."

"I bet it'll be more exciting than mine anyway. Mine will only be me and my mom and dad. You know, I don't have any real friends," Johnny said, giving Casey a rueful look.

Casey squeezed his arm, and gave him a warm smile. "You have one now."

Johnny cheered up. "That's right, I do, don't I?"

"So, what did you do yesterday?"

Not mentioning that he had moped around for much of the day, Johnny told Casey about the other things he had read about her great-grandfather. As always, Casey listened intently, without interruption.

Johnny had just finished when his father spoke. "Pay attention, you two, the parade is almost here."

At his father's words both Johnny and Casey turned their attention to the street, where a ripple of cheering and clapping was coming from farther away. Soon, the first military personnel appeared and the cheering became louder, swelling in volume as the veterans appeared.

As the veterans wheeled smartly and came to a halt in their place beside the memorial, two things in particular struck Johnny. The first was how these aging men held themselves so upright, and second, the glittering array of medals pinned to every man's chest. But what impressed him the most was when a senior Legion member stepped up to the microphone and read John McCrae's poem "In Flanders Fields."

Johnny had never heard the poem before, or had any idea about when or where it had been written. But it had such an impact on him, he decided it would be something he would ask Casey about later.

Next came the laying of wreaths at the foot of the memorial by various dignitaries and military groups. Then a soldier stepped smartly forward and raised a bugle to his lips. Everyone fell silent as the strains of the "Last Post" filled the air.

After the two minutes' silence, a gun went off, signalling the end of the service, and the crowd began to disperse.

It was Johnny's father who spoke first, echoing what Casey had said to Johnny earlier. "Did anyone else notice during the two minutes' silence how all the veterans seemed to be staring at the sky, just as if they were back there somewhere, reliving some moment, some battle or maybe a fallen comrade? It made me think that if only we could go back, even for a brief time, we could understand so much more. But since that's impossible, I guess we just have to do the best we can with what we get from history."

Casey, who was walking alongside Johnny, squeezed his arm and winked, bringing a smile to his face.

Epilogue

MR. GUPTA SHUFFLED the papers on his desk for what seemed like an eternity as everyone in the class waited to hear what he had to say about their essays.

Finally, he cleared his throat and started speaking. "The essay that showed the most originality and was the best written, was, unquestionably, the one submitted by Jonathan Anders."

"Anders?" Jason Lee exploded, jumping to his feet. "I don't believe it."

Mr. Gupta frowned at Jason, then turned back to Johnny. "I don't know where you got the idea from, Johnny, but it was without a doubt very clever."

"The idea came from a friend, but the writing is all mine, sir." Johnny looked around defiantly at Jason, who was still standing with a look of utter disbelief on his face.

"I certainly hope so, because I am going to suggest something that requires you to be honest. At first I felt that this essay," the history teacher waved the sheaf of papers at the class, "was good enough for the school newspaper."

Johnny gasped, as Mr. Gupta continued. "But on second thought, I decided it really deserved to reach a wider audience. And my suggestion is that you send it off to a competition for new writers, or even to the magazine *Canada's History*. In fact, if you wish, I would be prepared to help you with that."

Johnny was so dumbstruck that all he could do was nod.

"Fine, then I'll see what I can do. In the meantime, you'd better look after this." Waving the papers again, Mr. Gupta signalled to Johnny to come up and collect his essay.

Then he continued, addressing the still shell-shocked class, "As for the rest of you, I don't want you to think that your essays were not up to standard. In fact, some were very good, and I've written my conclusions on each. Please come up and collect them now. Then you may leave."

As they left the classroom, Jason Lee fell into step with Johnny. "You'd better have written this yourself, Anders, because if it goes to one of those competitions and they find you didn't really write it, you'd better find another school before next term."

"Well, I did write it, Lee. Every word."

With that, Johnny rushed down the hallway and outside to where Casey was waiting anxiously. He took her completely by surprise as he raced down the steps, took her in his arms and spun her around and around with sheer delight, gasping as he shouted out his news.

ABOUT THE AUTHOR

Charles Reid, a Londoner by birth, spent his early years surviving the London Blitz. After a stint in Britain's Royal Navy, Charles returned to civilian life, both in his native England and in his adopted land, Canada. Upon retirement he decided to write for young people about the contribution made by previous generations to the cause of freedom. He started with the story of Willie McKnight, the fighter pilot whose exploits were revealed in *Hurricanes over London*. In this novel, he combined his own experiences of the turbulent war years of his childhood with those of this legendary fighter pilot, who became a hero to his generation. His next book, *Chasing the Arrow*, revealed the political mistakes that led to the demise of one of the world's great fighter planes, the Avro Arrow. His latest novel, *Ghost of Heroes Past*, covers both world wars and the Russian Revolution. Charles Reid makes his home in Lantzville, British Columbia, on the east coast of Vancouver Island.

Recycled
Supporting responsible use
of forest resources
FSC   www.fsc.org   Cert no. SGS-COC-003153
© 1996 Forest Stewardship Council

100%

MARQUIS
Marquis Book Printing Inc.

Québec, Canada
2010

Printed on Silva Enviro which contains 100% recycled post-consumer fibre,
is EcoLogo, Processed Chlorine Free and manufactured using biogas energy.